Ethan, Suspended

Ethan,
Suspended

Pamela Ehrenberg

Eerdmans Books for Young Readers
Grand Rapids, Michigan / Cambridge, U.K.

for Eric, the original E-man

Text © 2007 Pamela Ehrenberg

Published in 2007 by Eerdmans Books for Young Readers,
an imprint of Wm. B. Eerdmans Publishing Co.

Wm. B. Eerdmans Publishing Co.
2140 Oak Industrial Dr. NE, Grand Rapids, Michigan 49505
P.O. Box 163, Cambridge CB3 9PU U.K.

www.eerdmans.com/youngreaders

Manufactured in the United States of America

11 10 09 08 07   7 6 5 4 3 2 1

Library of Congress Cataloging-in-Publication Data
Ehrenberg, Pamela.
Ethan, suspended / written by Pamela Ehrenberg.
p.   cm.
Summary: With his parents separating and Ethan being suspended
from school, his parents send him to his grandparents in Washington D.C.
which is worlds apart from his home in a Philadelphia suburb.

ISBN 978-0-8028-5324-0 (hardcover: alk. paper)
[1. Grandparents — Fiction. 2. Friendship — Fiction. 3. Race relations —
Fiction. 4. Middle schools — Fiction. 5. Schools — Fiction.
6. Washington (D.C.) — Fiction.]   I. Title.

PZ7.E32345Et   2007
[Fic] — dc22

2006032697

Text type set in Adobe Garamond

Acknowledgments

Many thanks to Eerdmans editor Shannon White, for believing in Ethan from the beginning and working tirelessly to make his story so much better, as well as to Justin Lawrence and Ethan's other friends at Eerdmans. I am grateful to the following people for feedback and encouragement on drafts of the novel: Barbara Esstman, Rachel Givner, Gwen Glazer, Kirsten Green, Holly Jones, T. J. Lee, Phyllis Mass, Elizabeth McBride, Farrar Miles, Meredith Narcum Tseu, Don Sadowsky, Melissa Schiffman, Brooke Stanley, Chad Tanaka, and the Hardy Middle School book club. I remain deeply indebted to the students at Paul Junior High Public Charter School, who taught me so much more than I taught them. Finally, I am grateful to my family: Talia Ehrenberg, who was the very first to celebrate with me; Joan and David Grebow; Cousin Frank Watzman; Sylvia, Aaron, and Sarah Grebow; Randy and Ron Ehrenberg; Rachel, Jason, and Noah Ehrenberg; and

Faye Britt and the late Sam Britt. And of course, Eric, who gives me courage and strength for writing, for life, and for everything else.

Prologue

It feels like I'm running, faster than I've ever run before. Past the library and the Whole Foods, past Josh and Caleb and Tyler, who are running too, past everything in Maple Heights. I feel like I'm crossing Meadowfalls Road, coming up on I-76, almost out of sight.

But I'm not running. I'm standing still. My feet feel like they're glued to the sidewalk by giant wads of bubble gum.

I'm yelling. I'm standing over Alex Krashevsky, shouting, "Are you okay? Are you okay?" just like I learned in the first-aid class I took as a counselor-in-training at tennis camp.

"Ethan, come on!" Josh calls to me. He's on the other side of the parking lot, and I could catch up if I ran fast enough. If my feet weren't stuck to the ground.

But I can't move, and Alex Krashevsky, sprawled out on the bloodstained sidewalk, can't move, either. I hear a siren, but it sounds far away, like Alex and I are trapped inside a plastic snow globe, and everything else is happening outside.

I'm still yelling "Are you okay?" to Alex. I didn't learn much else in that first-aid class, because they said if we yelled loud enough, somebody would hear us and come to help.

1

"Ethan? Ethan! We're over here!"

I heard my grandmother's scratchy voice over the mobs of people in Union Station. At least, it sounded like my grandmother. It had been a while since I'd heard her voice on the phone. So far Washington, D.C., smelled like buttery pretzels and fresh-baked chocolate chip cookies. I was starving.

"What were you — the last person off the train?"

My grandmother's hair was redder than I remembered. She pulled me into an awkward hug and then licked her thumb and rubbed my cheek. Hard.

My grandfather nodded at me from behind his big, rectangular glasses.

"Let's get all this to the car," he said, pointing to my bag. "I don't want to get charged an extra hour for parking."

Thank God I would only be here a week, while I was

suspended from school. I picked up my bag and followed my grandparents past pizza and McDonald's. The cheese puffs I ate on the train were a distant memory, and my breakfast of frozen waffles with peanut butter might as well have been from another lifetime.

In the Union Station garage, we climbed into a blue Lincoln I had never seen. "Ellen, what did you do with the parking stub?" my grandfather asked.

"I don't have it. You never gave it to me."

"Oh, I gave it to you. You put it in that pocketbook, and when somebody needs it you don't know what you did with it."

"Oh, here," sighed my grandmother, pulling the parking stub out of the glove compartment.

On the way to their house, we passed a mini-mart, an All-for-a-Dollar store, and a takeout place selling pizza/sandwiches/Chinese/fried chicken. The sidewalks were gray and cracked. I watched a man in a dirty sweatshirt throw a cup into an overflowing trash can, then watched the cup bounce out. A woman limped down the street in a saggy dress with curlers in her hair. Maple Heights didn't have a "downtown," just Maple Heights Mall, where it was always seventy-two degrees and they waxed the floors a hundred times a day. Josh and Caleb and Tyler were probably eating Boardwalk Fries in the food court right at this very moment. I was starving. My mom was probably opening our shiny black refrigerator and helping herself to takeout leftovers: barbecue pork buns, Vietnamese summer rolls, chicken satay with peanut sauce. Could a person starve to death in a week?

At a red light, dressed-up people were spilling out of a big stone church. A little girl with braids stared into the window of our car like she had never seen a white family before. My grandfather honked the horn, and she jumped back. Across from the church, three guys in paint-splattered clothes were sitting on milk crates in front of a 7-11 store.

We turned a few corners and my grandfather slowed down and came to a stop. All the houses on the street had the same red brick and white siding, but one displayed Halloween decorations, more than a month early; another had a plastic playhouse out front; and another was partly hidden by a large row of bushes. My grandparents' house was the only one without something special outside — not that I was complaining. Did the little white Jewish couple really need to add anything to the outside of their house to stick out in this neighborhood?

I hoped to go inside unnoticed, but the man next door took a break from raking leaves to wave hello. He had a big smile and a Washington Redskins sweatshirt.

"Ethan!" he said, like I was a long-lost relative. "The last time I saw you, you were knee-high to a grasshopper."

"Ethan, you remember our neighbor Mr. Taylor," my grandmother said like it was a fact, but I didn't recognize the man at all. The last time we visited D.C., I was in first grade.

"Hi," I said.

"You might remember my boys, they are about your age. They're with their aunt today, or I would have sent them over as a welcoming committee."

"Oh."

"My daughter Kameka's inside, but she's sleeping." He put his finger to his lips like he didn't want to wake a baby. We waved goodbye and went inside.

By then I knew more about Mr. Taylor and his family than any of my neighbors back home. Well, any except the Krashevskys, but I was trying to forget them. I didn't want to remember Mr. Krashevsky giving me a ride to the bus, or Mrs. Krashevsky pushing her metal grocery cart down the street and waving hello when she saw me hitting tennis balls against the garage. Mostly, I didn't want to remember their son Alex, or the look on his face that day outside Maple Heights Middle School. I wanted to forget them all.

After lunch (vegetable soup, peanut butter sandwiches, and bananas, no dessert), my grandmother showed me where to put my stuff. I would be in my Uncle Ed's old room, the uncle I never met because he died before I was born.

The room had wood floors, with a faded blue rug in the middle and dark wood furniture. It had two little lamps and a framed diploma from Wilson High School, 1967. The closet was jammed full of old boxes. And when I sat on the bed, it sank in the middle. It was my first time sitting on a dead person's bed.

◀◀◀　▶▶▶

The whole house was like a time capsule, a perfectly preserved little world where nobody would want to live, definitely not for more than a week. Computers, cable TV, and most other things that required batteries or plugs might as well have never been invented.

I spent the first few days reading Lone Ranger comic books I found in a box in the closet. At first I felt weird reading a dead person's comic books, but I hadn't thought of bringing a book to read, and if you wanted to read a magazine at my grandparents' house, your choices were freebies from AARP or from the insurance company. Compared to those, the Lone Ranger was pretty good.

I called my mom once to say I had arrived safely, but she was on her way out to a meeting.

"On Saturday morning?" I asked.

"These clients are insane. They wanted to meet at eight, but I held them off 'til ten."

"Oh. Well, I guess I'll see you in a few days."

"Hmm."

"Well," I said, "probably those clients are wondering where you are."

"Probably," my mom sighed. "All right, I'll talk to you soon, sweetie."

After we hung up, I picked up another Lone Ranger comic.

〈〈〈   〉〉〉

On Sunday, I was bored and thirsty from the musty comic books so I wandered into the kitchen to see what my grandparents were doing. I almost wandered right back out. My grandmother was chopping raw fish, and my grandfather was organizing coupons from the newspaper, using a magnifying glass and a pair of special scissors from a plastic case.

When I walked in, my grandfather was saying, "At least if he was in high school, we'd have sports to go to. I guess they don't do much of that at the junior high."

Who were they kidding? We hadn't gotten *that* close in the past few days, not close enough for them to come to Maple Heights to watch me play sports.

"I play tennis in the spring," I said, trying to be polite.

He looked at me like I had said I was a ballet dancer. "Is that for boys who are too prissy for polo?"

Before I could answer, my grandmother interrupted. "Now, I don't think there's a tennis team at Parker, but otherwise it's a perfectly fine school."

"What's Parker?" I said. It sounded like fancy boarding school where kids rode horses to class.

"The junior high," my grandmother said. "It's at Eighth and Pennington, or is it Seventh? Do you know, Ira?"

"Seventh, Eighth, what's the difference? He'll walk with the Taylor kids next door. They know what block it's on."

Now I was picturing a city school with graffiti and fights and drug dealers. What did this school have to do with me? Could they think —

"I'm not going to school here," I said, confused. "I'm going back to Maple Heights next week."

My grandmother smiled at me like I was four years old, and my grandfather scowled like his coupon-clipping was messed up forever.

Then I had a terrible thought. Was my mom kicking me out for good? Could she even do that? Forget no video games, instant messaging, or cable TV. What about no friends, no normal food? She was taking away my family and my bed! And my school, which fed into Maple

Heights High School, where, like, ninety-nine percent of graduates went to four-year colleges. Didn't anyone care about my education? Forget being grounded, this was imprisonment, solitary confinement, torture.

"No. I won't do it!" I shouted.

No response.

"Will someone please tell me what is going on?" I asked softly, trying to be nicer.

When nobody answered, I grabbed the nearest coupon, which was for Progresso soup, and threw it on the ground. It fluttered down gently, and nobody said anything for a long time. Finally, I picked it up, slammed it on the table, and ran upstairs.

I heard my grandfather mutter, "One interruption after another. People must think these coupons sort themselves."

In my uncle's room I noticed a plastic bag on the dresser, a big white bag that said "ValuBuy" in orange letters. Inside I found two pairs of navy pants, two white dress shirts, a navy sweater, five pairs of dress socks, and a pair of ridiculous, shiny loafers. On top was a note that was the biggest insult of all: *Dear Ethan, Try not to outgrow them all too soon. Love, Grandma and Grandpa.*

This was crazy! Being forced to go to a city school for who knows how long, for one stupid afternoon that Josh and Caleb and Tyler hadn't even lost TV privileges over?

There was no way. And my grandparents couldn't possibly think I would agree to wear a uniform to school, especially with penny loafers.

On the hall telephone, I dialed my mom's number. And I mean, really dialed, on the kind of phone you spin around in a circle with your finger instead of pushing buttons. It sat on a round wooden table with a shelf underneath. Visiting here was like traveling back in time.

"Ethan, what a nice surprise!" said my mom, like I was a friend she bumped into at Whole Foods.

"What am I doing here?"

"What do you mean, sweetie? Did something happen?"

"*Nothing's* happened. Nothing ever happens here, unless you count chopping fish and cutting coupons. How long are you planning on me staying here?"

"Ethan, we talked about this. We said things might take time to settle down — "

"No, *you* said things might take time, and when I said, *Like a week?* you said, *Let's see how things are going.*" I mean, how long could people keep giving her dirty looks at the dry cleaner's?

"Right, that's exactly — "

"Grandma and Grandpa think I'm going to school here!" I yelled. "They bought me a uniform! With penny loafers! Can you talk to them?"

There was a pause, or more like half a pause.

"You know, some kids like having uniforms so they don't have to decide what to wear to school every day."

"Well, good for them. But I'm not going to school here."

Then my mom said, "Well, I guess I thought we had talked about that possibility."

"What? No, we did not talk about that possibility." She did that to me all the time, got busy with work and then said, "Oh, I thought I mentioned I couldn't pick you up today," or, "Oh, I thought I told you your appointment changed." That's what happened that day with Alex Krashevsky. I was waiting around after school because nobody told me my orthodontist appointment had changed.

When my mom didn't answer, I added, "How is living with Grandma and Grandpa possibly going to help me? I don't even know them! And I know what you think about this neighborhood — that's why you had us stay in a hotel the one time we visited."

"You remember that?"

"I remember lots of things." When she didn't answer, I kept going. "Has anyone even talked to Dad about this? Why can't I live with him?"

It was the first time I admitted out loud that, technically, my dad didn't live at our house anymore. After tennis camp in July, I had gone to computer animation camp, and then our family was supposed to go to the shore like we did every summer. Instead my parents sat us down at the kitchen table and said they were going to try being separated. I said it sounded like what they were already trying, which was never being home at the same time anyway. My sister Margo had kicked me under the table.

They had ordered a pizza for dinner, but the pizza guys never came, which was okay because I might have stopped liking pizza forever if I had connected it with that night. Margo said it was inconsiderate to split up when she was starting college across the country and needed a home to come back to. But I said I wouldn't complain if they waited until I left for college, so why didn't Margo shut up and think about somebody else for a change? My parents just sat there, letting us yell at each other, and a few days later my dad moved into an apartment in Old City, Philadelphia. I haven't seen it yet. By choice. I've refused to talk to him since he moved out. So living with Dad wasn't exactly my top choice, but it had to be better than living at my grandparents' house.

"He works late, honey," my mom said.

"So? At least he doesn't chop up raw fish! At least he doesn't take two hours on a Sunday to cut out coupons with special scissors!"

"True," said my mom. "But he just — didn't think it would work for right now."

"So you asked him?"

"Yes."

"If I could live there?"

"We talked about it."

"And he said 'no'."

"He . . . didn't think now was the best time."

"And it's not the best time for you either, right? You need things to 'settle down'?"

My mom didn't answer.

"Fine! I hope you get sick on chicken satay!" I yelled before slamming down the phone.

When I turned around, my grandfather was standing close behind me. "That's not free, you know, long-distance calling," he said.

"I know," I said. "I just — had to ask her something."

"Mmm . . . Next time, if you're going to yell that loud, see if she can hear you without the phone. Just stand on the front step and yell. Leave Ma Bell out of it."

Whoever Ma Bell was. The corners of his eyes looked like they might be smiling, but I wasn't sure.

In Uncle Ed's room, I unzipped and zipped my duffel bag a few times, listening to the rhythm it made against the quiet. I was stuck. I looked at the stuff from ValuBuy, felt the saggy mattress underneath me, and smelled fish cooking downstairs. The most important thing was not to cry, and the second-most-important thing was not to think about Maple Heights. I was in a whole new place, where I could pretend my parents still lived together and nobody knew about the mess that landed me here.

Maybe a saggy mattress would be a small price to pay.

2

The next morning, I ate cereal from a plastic bowl decorated with brown and yellow flowers. I put on my scratchy new uniform. I was rubbing my shoes together, trying to make them stop squeaking, when the doorbell rang.

Two kids dressed like me were standing on our front step. They had dark skin like their dad and the same skin-close haircut.

"Hi, Ethan! Hi, Ms. L.!" said the shorter one. The taller one nodded hello.

"I'm Felix," the shorter one told me, "and this is my brother Daron. I'm in seventh grade and he's in ninth. He don't talk much. I mean, he doesn't talk much, but if you ever need anything at school, Daron is the person to see."

"Okay," I said. "Thanks."

"You all have a good day," my grandmother said. She had gotten up early to make me breakfast and was standing in the doorway fidgeting with an orange dishtowel.

On our way to school, Felix made sure I was between him and his brother, like they were bringing me in for show-and-tell. I hated being the new kid, especially since it was already the second month of school.

"I never met a kid from Philadelphia before," Felix said. "Where in Philadelphia you from, anyway?"

"It's near Philadelphia. A suburb called Maple Heights."

"Ohhh," Felix said. "My dad said you was from Philadelphia, and I asked which part but he didn't know. That explains why, 'cause you ain't really from Philadelphia, just near Philadelphia."

"Felix," said Daron, "give the kid some peace."

Felix glared at Daron and told me, "Don't worry about him. He's just grumpy in the morning. He don't really cheer up until ten or eleven a.m. Not me, though. I've been up since six watching cartoons. What cartoons do you like?"

"Well, I sometimes watch this one called Space Monsters," I admitted, hoping Space Monsters wasn't too dorky for D.C.

"Whoa, I don't think we get that here," said Felix. "What's it like?"

While I talked about Space Monsters, my feet started to hurt in the penny loafers. After a block and a half, my feet were on fire. I kicked a soda bottle onto somebody's yard, but it only made my toes hurt more.

At school, we waited outside on the parking lot, which was also a basketball court, until it was time to go in. Most of the kids were black, except for a few Latinos. Everyone wore navy blue pants or skirts, and the kids without jackets were all wearing white shirts. This was crazy — a public school in the middle of the city where the kids were dressed like it was a fancy boarding school in New England or someplace. Even though we were all dressed alike, I felt stares from every direction.

I tried to send a telepathic message to my grandparents. *Get me out of here, and you can go back to your coupon-clipping routine. I'll even clip coupons for you! I'll chop fish!*

"What you don't want to do," Felix was explaining, "is get too friendly with the Spanish kids. Usually they leave us alone and we leave them alone and everything's okay. It's when people get too friendly that problems get started. Ain't that right, Daron?"

But Daron was shuffling over to a group of guys.

"What kind of problems?" I asked Felix, but kids had started moving toward the door, and Felix and I got separated. I was caught in a mob of tall kids, short kids, fat kids, a few skinny kids. A pretty girl near me was wearing a navy skirt with one red sock and one purple sock. The mob pushed me forward into my first day at Parker Junior High.

❮❮❮ ❯❯❯

Without Felix, I stood out a lot more. Not just because of my skin color, but because I didn't know where my classes were, or which desk to sit in. My uniform felt stiff and new, like a costume. Nobody talked to me all morning, but I could tell the whole school was watching, waiting for me to do something stupid.

In the bathroom, some kids I didn't know laughed when they saw me jiggle the soap machine and reach up into the paper towel dispenser. Why was it funny to think the bathroom would have soap and paper towels?

By lunchtime, I was starving. I was good at combination locks, but these lockers were so old that you had to line the numbers up exactly and give the handle an extra push. Even then it would sometimes stick and you'd have to start over. All around me, lockers banged open and slammed shut. What if lunch ended before I got my locker open?

Finally the locker clicked and I pulled my lunch from the shelf. My grandmother had packed it in a white plastic bag from the supermarket, all crinkled from being stored in an old Kleenex box. I hadn't paid much attention to it in the morning, but now I couldn't imagine walking through the halls with it, letting other kids see how my grandparents lived. My face was burning. I shoved my lunch down far into my backpack and turned around.

A girl was behind me. She was taller than me, with sparkly purple glasses and a navy blue skirt that swished around her knees. She had medium-brown skin and black hair pulled back from her face. Then I saw she had one red sock and one purple sock — she was the same girl I had been squished up near in the crowd coming in that morning.

All around us, lockers slammed and kids yelled to their friends, but she just stood there, holding her books in front of her chest. She smiled at me.

"Uh, hi," I said. It was the first thing I had said out loud inside Parker Junior High.

"Hi," she said.

We stood there a long time. I couldn't imagine what someone like her — sophisticated- and smart-looking — would want with me, so I stood there and waited. She had a nice smile, and her lips were shiny.

She pointed to the locker next to mine and said, "Um, my locker . . ."

Sure, her locker. The one whose door was blocked by my backpack lying on the ground. I picked it up.

"Sorry," I said.

"No problem."

Idiot! How could I think she had something to say to me?

I followed the swarm of eighth-graders to the cafeteria. Felix's grade had already eaten, and Daron's grade was still in class. Most kids were waiting in line for hot food, so there were plenty of empty tables. I picked one and sat down, and then I set my backpack on the table to hide my lunch.

My lunch was all old-people food: a cream cheese sandwich on rye bread, a bag of carrot sticks, an apple, pretzels, oatmeal cookies, and a can of store-brand ginger ale. What kid drank ginger ale, especially store brand? I didn't know which was worse: eating this food or being seen with it. But I didn't have any money with me, so it was my only hope for staying conscious until 3:15.

My mouth was full of cream cheese and rye bread when three Latino kids (or Spanish, like Felix had said) came to the table. They all had lasagna, milk, green beans, and strawberry ice cream on a stick. A knot formed in my stomach where my appetite had been. The three guys sat down, surrounding me, and started eating. They didn't say anything, but they kept glancing at me between bites. I remembered what Felix had said about not getting friendly with Spanish kids, but they didn't seem very talkative. What would these guys do to me anyway?

Finally, one of them said, "Your name still Ethan?"

So far that morning, three teachers had introduced me in class.

"Yeah," I said, trying not to squeak. The guy talking to me was my height but skinnier, with a big mess of black hair. His white shirt looked thin, like it had been washed a lot.

He explained to his friends, "Ethan's with me in the egghead classes. Hey, Ethan, how come you in the egghead classes?"

"Uh, I don't know." I didn't know I was in egghead classes. Whatever those were.

"Me either," the kid said, laughing. "Most days I wake up and I'm saying, 'What the hell am I doing here?'"

"Hey, Diego, talking about what the hell is someone doing here . . .," one of the other guys said to the kid who recognized me from class. This guy was bigger, with a round face and a mouth full of lasagna that tried to escape when he laughed.

"Yeah," said the third kid, looking at me. "Did you tell him he could sit here?"

Diego shrugged.

"I don't gotta tell him nothing."

"I don't know if I like people sitting someplace uninvited," said the bigger guy.

I should have said, *I don't know if I like people who spit lasagna when they talk.* That's what the old Ethan, back in

Maple Heights, would have said, and everyone would have laughed. But this new Ethan was less funny, and less brave.

I stood up.

"I gotta go anyway. I gotta . . . do some stuff about my schedule."

"Whatever," Diego said. His friends watched me as I left the cafeteria, and I still felt their eyes on me when I sat down on the stairs with the rest of my lunch.

The stairs felt cool and smooth when I touched them, worn down from, like, a hundred years of kids' feet. But in a hundred years, I was probably the first kid to sit there with a cream cheese sandwich and store-brand ginger ale.

3

"Why waste money on special bags just to hold your lunch?" my grandmother said when I asked her about using a brown paper bag. "That's how your generation expects the world to be, use something once and be done with it."

With my old-people lunches in wrinkled plastic bags, I was basically a freak of nature at Parker Junior High. Like, "Come see the kid with seven heads" or, "Come see the kid who's alive in a jar." Everything I did — opening my locker, turning in homework, drinking from the water fountain — was so freakish the whole school had to stare. I didn't even have to do anything stupid like trip or spill food. Just by being myself, I was the most ridiculous person alive.

In my second week at Parker, during our "Mathercize" warm-up, a kid named Lyle who sat in front of me farted. It was the kind you could both hear and smell if you were close enough, and a few kids near us giggled. Even I was smiling, until Lyle looked around and pointed at me. Everyone laughed even harder, and the girl next to me, Janeen, put her hand in the air.

"Mrs. Franklin, can I move my seat? Ethan is disturbing me." Janeen gave me a look like I not only had farted, but I was also spreading a contagious farting disease.

Two rows ahead of me, Diego was drawing or coloring something at his desk. He was smiling, but whether that was about his picture, or what was happening to me, or the general topic of farting, I couldn't tell.

Mrs. Franklin sighed. "You may not move your seat," she told Janeen, "but you and the rest of the class may put your names on your Mathercize and pass them to the front of the room. This will count as a pop quiz in your quiz grade."

Everyone complained as notebooks opened and papers moved forward. I heard my name under a couple of people's breath, and the word "cracker."

Somebody said, "We never had pop quizzes until *he* came to this school."

Three days in a row now, I had found fresh Saltine cracker crumbs at the bottom of my locker. Plus these two guys, Nate and Kennard, were constantly reaching behind me and untucking the back of my shirt. Back home, my shirt would have been untucked anyway, but here shirts had to be tucked in. Kids actually got in trouble over it. When I told them to stop, they laughed. This went on about a week, until our social studies teacher, Mr. Kirk, saw Nate untuck my shirt in the hallway.

Mr. Kirk called us both over and leaned down close to our faces. In a quiet voice, he said, "Nate, what you do on your own time is your own business. But here in school, I have seen rumors get started about what it means when a guy likes to undress another guy — "

"What?" Nate interrupted, much louder than Mr. Kirk had been talking. "I ain't trying to — " he lowered his voice. "No way I be undressing nobody!"

Mr. Kirk continued. "To prevent misunderstandings then, I suggest you keep your hands off other students' clothing. Am I understood?"

"Yeah."

"I said, am I understood?"

"Yeah! I mean, yes."

Mr. Kirk stood up straight. "Get out of here. You're both going to be late for class."

At Maple Heights Middle School, I used to get in trouble for making other kids snarf chocolate milk out their noses. I came up with funny answers in class and once turned in a twenty-line poem where every line rhymed with "tuba." I wasn't the most popular kid at school, but I was friends with the popular kids, so I could pretty much be myself. I never realized how lucky I was.

After another week of eating lunch on the stairs, a teacher I didn't recognize told me I had to eat in the cafeteria with everyone else. I put the rest of my chicken salad sandwich back in one of those plastic bags that vegetables come in, and I took my sandwich, apple, and banana back into the cafeteria.

I didn't look for anyone I knew, since I would have to see them all afternoon after they laughed me out of a seat. Maybe kids I didn't know would ignore me. I could even pretend I didn't speak English, that I was a foreign exchange student. That would explain the weird lunch. I tried to think of what places more exotic than Pennsylvania had people who looked white: Albania? Latvia? Someplace where my name would have a lot of consonants.

I sat down near four girls who were busy with a conversation. Their voices got quieter after I sat down, until one of them said, in terrible Spanish, "Ho-la! Como se llaaaama?"

When I didn't answer, everyone laughed hysterically.

"Told you!" one of them sang to the rest of the group. "Told you he wasn't Spanish."

Eight eyes were fixed on me. At least one of the girls

was lighter-skinned than I had been after two weeks at tennis camp.

"I don't think he's a albino," one of them said slowly, "'cause wouldn't his eyes be all pink?"

They giggled again.

"Kanisha thinks he's a albino," one of them said.

"No, I said he's *not* a albino."

"So what is he?"

"What are you?" one of them asked me.

When I didn't answer, one of them said, "Maybe he's from a different country. Maybe he don't talk English."

Yes, I thought, *yes!* I cautiously took a bite of my sandwich.

"Or Spanish," one of the girls said, before collapsing into laughter. She squirted a Go-gurt into her mouth.

"I think he's just a regular white person," said one of her friends. "A European American."

"Why would a white person come to this school?"

"Maybe he's a narc."

More laughter.

"Yeah, the cops send somebody to blend in with the students, only they forget and send a white kid." She hiccupped from laughing so hard. One of her friends patted her on the back and offered her some juice.

I shoved some banana in my mouth and stood up to throw away my trash.

Classes were okay when the other kids left me alone. The best one was social studies. Mr. Kirk took my picture and added it to the row of Polaroids (one of each of his students) that went all the way around the room. I was the lightest-skinned kid, of course, but they were up so high you didn't really notice. My schedule said the class was on Washington, D.C., history, but on my first day, we watched broadcasts of Martin Luther King, Jr., speeches from the 1960s, and analyzed what made them persuasive. In Maple Heights, school was closed every year for Martin Luther King, Jr.'s birthday, or the Monday closest to his birthday, but I had never heard his speeches. I thought they were persuasive because they weren't boring; they were something you'd actually want to listen to.

When I told Felix and Daron about social studies and Mr. Kirk, Daron said, "You're lucky. People say he's good."

"How come?"

Daron shrugged.

"He just makes it interesting, not like the lady I had last year for D.C. History. I hear he goes backwards, starting with the present and going back to the Indians."

"Oh, so that's why we're on Martin Luther King in October."

Daron nodded.

"Yeah, I heard he does a lot of civil rights."

Felix had been working on wiggling his ears. He stopped to say, "Man, if you know so much about civil rights, how come we gotta wear our shirts tucked in all the time? I got written up last week 'cause my stupid shirt keeps coming untucked."

My stupid shirt kept doing that too.

〈〈〈   〉〉〉

That afternoon my grandmother met me at the door with a hot pink envelope.

"You got a letter from your sister," she said.

I saw Margo's handwriting on the back, and the address of her dorm in silver gel pen. I hardly ever got mail at home, other than *Sports Illustrated Kids*, which I didn't think would find me here.

The table was already set for supper, and my grandfather was working on the crossword from the newspaper.

"And your mother called," he said without looking up.

"Really?"

"From her office," he said. "Daytime phone rates! She said the firm doesn't mind her making long-distance calls, but I say a firm that doesn't mind that is a firm won't be in business very long."

"What did she say?" I asked. I looked from my grandfather to my grandmother and back again, but neither of

30

them seemed to remember anything about the call except what it had cost.

"She's fine," my grandmother said. "Though she hardly got a word out, with your grandfather going on about the phone rates."

"Now, wait a minute, I wasn't —"

"Why don't you see what your sister has to say?" my grandmother said to me. "At least nobody can interrupt her in a letter."

"Are you saying that I interrupt?" my grandfather said.

I left the two of them arguing and took Margo's envelope upstairs. Inside was a piece of pink paper that she'd written on with the same silver gel pen she used on the envelope. I had to keep tilting the page to read what she wrote.

October 7

Dear Ethan-underneathen,

I started to forward you an email just now (a quasi-dirty joke from Uncle Frank, who at 93 really should know better, but what can I say, it was funny) — and then I realized I didn't know if you could check your email down there. Now that I think of it, do Grandma and Grandpa even have a computer? I remember when we visited, they tried to convince

31

Mom that microwave ovens had deadly radioactive consequences.

I can't believe I've been in college a month. Do you ever feel like you're on another planet? The volleyball team goes on a road trip tomorrow night and I'm covering it for the paper. Oh, and I'm thinking of doing this tutoring thing at a school near here. I'll fill you in more later.

Write me soon!

Love,

Margo Embargo

At first I wondered why I didn't feel happier to hear from her, but then I realized: I was hoping she would tell me news about home, fill me in about what was happening to my family. Could my parents be giving up on the whole separation idea? Either Margo was keeping a secret, or she was as clueless as I was. I put the letter in the top drawer of my uncle's desk, the first personal thing I had in my room in Washington.

4

One Friday after Social Studies, Diego said, "Art's gotta be the stupidest class ever invented."

I looked around to see who he was talking to, but nobody looked at him or responded. I hated art class, too. Kids were always running around with friends throwing things, which made my aloneness more obvious.

"We never do nothing," Diego went on. "Ms. Samson's always like, 'Okay, who remembers primary and secondary colors?' But half the class is talking and the other half won't even sit down, so by the time she takes out the art stuff we have, like, five minutes until it's time to leave."

He seemed to be talking to me.

"What do you do over by the window?" I asked.

He grinned.

"You noticed that? Especially, like, at the end of class? Because you can see out the window to Garfield High School, where my brother and my cousins go. When they leave school, I like to wave out the window and try to make them see me."

"So everybody has to take art?" I said as we left the classroom. At Maple Heights Middle School, you got to choose between band, chorus, and art, and I had played clarinet in the band.

"Yeah," Diego said. "Except the kids in jazz band. We need a boycott or something, like all of us going somewhere besides the art room. But the only other place to go is jazz band."

"I could be in jazz band. I play clarinet," I said. I was immediately sorry I said it. Diego was only the fourth person I had talked to in this school, and I didn't want him thinking I was a band nerd.

But he looked impressed.

"You gotta tell Ms. Samson," he said. "Tell her you belong in jazz band and you gotta see Mr. Harper. Room 103. Just tell her, and she'll write you a pass."

"But why — "

"You can be the first kid to boycott!"

I didn't have time to argue, because we had reached the art room. Kids were sitting on the desks and leaning on the big utility sink in the back of the room. One guy was playing his Game Boy under a desk. He hadn't even bothered turning the sound off.

Diego took me to the front of the room, where the

34

teacher was looking for something on her desk. He didn't give me a chance to say the things he had told me to say — he just started talking to the teacher.

"Ms. Samson, hi. This is Ethan and he's new. He's from — where are you from, again?"

"Pennsylvania."

"Yeah. It's like, only his third week here at school. But he's not supposed to be in art, he's supposed to be in jazz band. Can you please write him a pass to the band room?"

Two minutes later, I was in the hall with my backpack and a blue sticky-note that said "Ethan to band." What room had Diego said? 203? 301? The class in 301 looked like they were sitting at desks, so I went downstairs to 203, but those kids were at desks too. One of them saw me and waved, but the teacher shut the door before I could wave back.

I walked around the first floor until I heard noise that didn't sound like a math or English class. When I peeked through the door crack into room 103, I saw ten kids blowing into different instruments. I walked in. The room smelled like radiator steam and disinfectant. In front, trying to fix a music stand was a tall, skinny white guy with long gray hair growing in every direction.

"Hi," I said to him. "Uh, I'm Ethan Oppenheimer, and I'm new. I think I'm supposed to be in jazz band."

"Oh, you think so?" he said with an accent that wasn't

quite British. He looked up from the broken music stand and talked loudly over the musicians.

"You're ready to join this charming group of fine musicians who do their darnedest to sound like a herd of wild antelopes in questionable health?"

I couldn't help smiling.

"I guess," I said.

He smiled back.

"So, what instrument do you purport to play?"

"Uh, the clarinet," I said.

"I see," said the not-quite-British music teacher. "And your clarinet would be in your backpack, perhaps? Or in your pencil box?"

"Actually, it would be in Maple Heights, Pennsylvania," I said. "I mean, I know how to play, but I didn't bring my instrument with me when I switched schools."

He sighed. "Well, I'm sure your clarinet is having a fine time. Pennsylvania is lovely in the autumn," he said. "But sadly, both our school clarinets are on loan. You may, in fact, play the clarinet, but you do not play the clarinet in the Parker jazz band."

"Oh," I said. "Well, thanks anyway." I turned to go back upstairs to art. The teacher might not even remember I had been gone.

"However," he went on, "we do have a perfectly good

36

oboe sitting unused in a storage closet. Have you any interest in playing the oboe?"

An oboe in jazz band? "Well, I've never played it before."

"That was not the question, Mr. Oppenheimer."

"Do they write jazz music for oboes?"

"Also not the question — and as you can see, I do have a class to teach."

I said quickly, "If you can teach me oboe, I'll play."

He put his hand in the air and the warming-up musicians got quiet.

"Ladies and gentlemen," he said, "I would like you to meet Mr. Ethan Oppenheimer, the world's first jazz oboist."

I gave a little smile. "Hi," I said.

"I am Mr. Harper," he answered. "And this," he gestured to the kids sitting with their instruments, "is the Parker Jazz Band."

Even I knew the oboe wasn't a jazz instrument. But if Mr. Harper didn't mind, I'd rather stay there than go to art class, especially since Diego thought jazz band was cool. Or at least cooler than art.

Someone got the oboe from the storage room. The case was scratched and dusty, like it had waited a long time for someone to play it.

The girl behind me had her long legs stretched out

between the chairs, and I recognized her mismatched socks. I turned around, and the girl from the lockers smiled at me.

"Hi," she said.

"Hi."

She was holding her trombone on her lap. I had never seen a girl play a trombone before. I had never seen an oboe up close at all.

While everybody else practiced scales, Mr. Harper showed me how to put the oboe together and how to put the reed in my mouth. I blew into it, and sound came out on my second try. You had to use both lips on the oboe. It sounded more grown-up than the clarinet, like it had been around longer, and had a few more experiences.

"Not bad," Mr. Harper said, "for your first time holding an oboe. Can you come after school so I can show you fingering? We might just get you caught up in time for our December concert to feature the world's first jazz oboe!" (I think that was what he said, over the noise of everyone playing scales.)

"Uh, okay."

The band played "In the Mood" all the way through. Then one section at a time: the brass, wind, and percussion.

"Focus, percussion!" Mr. Harper yelled. "Trumpets, put some soul into it!"

For the first time since I'd been at Parker, nobody stared at me. I don't think anyone would have noticed if I had three arms, unless my elbow knocked into their instrument.

When the girl with red and purple socks played, the muscles in her legs stretched tight. Above her socks, she had wide, smooth, dark skin.

In the hall after class, she said, "Bet you've never see a girl play the trombone before."

"No, how'd you know?"

She shrugged.

"Most people haven't. But trombone-playing runs in my family."

"I didn't know there was a gene for that."

She looked at me like I was stupid.

"I didn't say there was a gene for it. I said it runs in my family. My grandfather played and then my father played, and now it's my turn. That's my father's instrument in there."

"Doesn't he need it?" I said, and then she gave me a look like I was definitely stupid.

"He's dead."

Oh.

"I'm Sharita. How did you end up at this school, anyway?"

Sharita. That was nice.

39

"My grandparents live around the corner," I said. "They've lived there for, like, fifty years."

"Really? How come?"

I shrugged. Why did my grandparents do anything?

"They're pretty stubborn."

"I know how that is," she said.

After school, Mr. Harper showed me how to move my fingers on the oboe to make specific notes, not just random sounds. He gave me an empty film canister that I could fill with water to keep the reed wet, and a piece of cigarette paper to slide under the keys to get spit out. I promised to come back for more help on Monday, and I tried not to think about what kids at my old school would say if they knew I was taking remedial oboe after school. I had to sign a form promising to bring the oboe back in good condition, and then Mr. Harper let me take the oboe home. I mean, to my grandparents' house.

As I was leaving school, Diego appeared from behind a row of lockers.

"Hey, E-man," he said. "What you still doing here?"

"I got into jazz band," I said, showing him the oboe case. "I'm learning to play oboe."

"Oboe!" he said. "What kind of jazz instrument's a oboe?"

"They were out of clarinets."

At lunch with his friends, I worried that Diego would beat me up, but now he wanted to know about oboes?

"Man," he said, shaking his head. "A oboe. Which way you walking?"

"Up Ninth Street to Tillerman Avenue," I said. "You?"

"I walk up Ninth Street a ways, too," he said. "You live close! How come you live so close?"

I shrugged.

"That's just where my grandparents live."

Diego and I walked together until I turned down Tillerman Avenue. Outside the Taylors' house, Daron was shoveling leaf piles into plastic bags, and Kameka was jumping in the piles. Felix was sweeping the sidewalk.

"Ethan!" he yelled when he saw me. "Where were you? We waited for you for, like, an hour!"

I looked at my watch. I had spent an hour with Mr. Harper and fifteen minutes walking home with Diego.

Felix corrected himself. "Okay, maybe not an hour, but a really long time. We would have waited longer, but we get in trouble if we don't come right home from school! Man, I hope you don't get your butt whupped."

In Maple Heights, I was used to being the first one home in the afternoon and not having anyone notice what time I got in. But of course my grandparents would know what time it was from the TV schedule.

"Sorry you waited," I told Felix, showing him my oboe

41

case. "I joined the jazz band, and I stayed after school so Mr. Harper could teach me the oboe."

"Cool," said Felix. "Can I play it sometime?"

"Maybe."

"It's good you got that as evidence," he said. "Last year, I used to talk a lot and I had to stay after school all the time. Then I came home late and my dad knew I was bad, so I got my butt whupped on top of staying after. But this year I've been good. I got six teachers, and so far only two of them called my dad about me talking too much."

"Yeah, but now you talk five times as much at home to make up for it," Daron said.

Felix grinned.

"So? At home I can talk all I want as long as I don't interrupt nobody's homework." He turned to me. "Everybody at our house does homework. Did you know our dad's getting a master's degree? He already went to college, but now he's going back for more school so he gets more money at his job, and maybe I get a new X-Box for Christmas."

"Hey, Ethan," Daron said, coming over to us, "who was that kid you were walking with?"

"A kid in my class," I said. "His name's Diego."

Daron let out a long, slow breath, and scrunched up his forehead.

"Well, I ain't telling you who to be friends with," he said. "Just be careful, that's all I'm saying."

"Why?" I remembered what they said about not getting too friendly with Spanish kids, but they didn't know Diego was practically the only other kid who talked to me at school.

"Daron don't really like Spanish kids," Felix said. "Ever since our mom — "

"It ain't that!" Daron interrupted. "I just seen that kid before, and I think Ethan should be careful."

"Well, I think you should put them leaves in some bags before Kameka spreads them all over the neighborhood," said Felix. Kameka had gotten bored sitting in the leaves, now that Daron wasn't trying to stop her, and she was running from pile to pile, throwing handfuls into the air.

"Oh, man," said Daron.

"I guess I should go inside," I said.

"Good luck not getting a butt whupping," said Felix.

Before I could ring the doorbell, my grandmother opened the door with a worried frown. She was wearing a yellow apron and carrying a can of frozen orange juice concentrate and a wooden spoon.

"Where on God's earth have you been?" she asked me, standing in the doorway so I couldn't enter the house.

"At school," I said. "The band teacher is going to teach

me the oboe after school." I showed her the oboe case in my hand.

She glared at me, but let me inside. My grandfather was standing next to the wooden mail and key holder, looking pale.

"I don't know where you think you are, that you can just come and go anytime you please," he said.

"Those Taylor boys were home over an hour ago," my grandmother said. "I don't think we need to remind you you're not in Maple Heights, Pennsylvania, anymore."

"I know."

"Maybe your parents let you run around all night, but it's not going to be that way here," she said.

Without meaning to, I said, "Four-thirty isn't all night."

"Are you talking back to me?" she snapped.

I shook my head. She still had the wooden spoon in her hand, covered with orange goop. No way would she hit me. The only time I ever got spanked, I was about Kameka's age and I had run down our street barefoot to chase the ice cream truck.

"From now on," my grandmother said, "you leave for school in the morning with the Taylor boys, and you come straight home when school is out. Do I make myself clear?"

I nodded. I didn't know how to ask about the oboe without sounding like I was talking back.

"What?" she said, looking straight at me. "Go ahead, ask your question now rather than regret it later."

I glanced at my grandfather. "Just ask already," he said. "Some of us care that our dinners are getting cold, and we like to be finished in time for the six o'clock news."

"Well," I said, "he lent me this oboe, and he wants me to learn how to play after school."

"Who's this 'he'?" my grandmother asked.

"The band teacher. Mr. Harper. He's going to help me play good enough for the concert in December."

"*Well* enough," my grandmother said. "*Well* is the adverb of good; it describes how you're going to play."

"Good enough or well enough, I've never heard of an oboe in a jazz band," my grandfather said.

"Can I do it?"

My grandmother sighed. "Have this Mr. . . ."

"Harper."

"Have this Mr. Harper call me on Monday. I want to know what days you'll be practicing and for how long."

"Okay," I said. "Thanks."

"Go wash your hands for supper. Front and back."

After we ate I practiced the oboe for half an hour. I sat on the edge of my uncle's bed with the vinyl shades all the way up, letting in the last bits of daylight.

45

The house was so hot I was wearing just a T-shirt and a pair of my Uncle Ed's old gym shorts. The longer I stayed in his room, the less he seemed like a creepy dead guy, and the more he felt like a regular uncle. The brown blanket was soft under my legs, which swung back and forth while I played. Or tried to play. My scales kept going off track because I was thinking about what Daron said about Diego and the Spanish kids. Why did he tell me to be careful?

It was hard to wonder and also keep track of my fingering, so half the time random notes came out. But then I remembered the deep, brassy notes from Sharita's trombone, and the smooth leg muscles that tensed up when she played. A jolt of energy raced through my body and the oboe, and suddenly I didn't think the music sounded too terrible for my first day.

5

Back home, I was always around other people. If I wasn't involved in an organized activity like tennis or computer camp, I was hanging out at a friend's house or meeting people at the arcade, or the food court, or the stadium-seating movie theater. Being home alone was boring, with my parents always working and Margo at school a hundred hours a day for plays and yearbook and extra-curricular activities. And then, after my dad and Margo left and my mom just kind of moped around, being home alone was even quieter and more depressing than usual. But that was nothing compared to being alone in my grandparents' house.

My mom called once a week, but always when I was in school. It was just like her — acting like she wanted to know how I was doing, but not actually wanting to talk to me. My friends back home were probably emailing to see how I was doing and saying they were sorry for how they treated me. They'd be even sorrier when I didn't answer their emails. It almost made me glad I was in a time-warp world without the Internet.

I spent a lot of time on the bedroom floor reading my uncle's comic books. He had a huge collection: Lone Ranger, Popeye, Looney Tunes, and some called Joe Palooka, about a boxer. I liked the ads in the back where you could send in money and get sea monkeys or toy soldiers. Uncle Ed hadn't torn any of them out, which made sense. I could imagine my grandfather lecturing him about the value of a nickel.

My uncle had died a long time ago, when he was twenty, from a bad reaction to some medicine. Which was too bad, because with my dad getting further and further out of my life and my grandfather complaining about coupons and parking spots, I imagined that my uncle would have been the most normal male relative I had. My mom hadn't talked about him much, just like she didn't really talk about anyone in her family. Back home I had never found that strange. But now that I was here, staying next to my mom's old room, sleeping in a bed that belonged to my dead uncle, it seemed like I should have known more about this side of the family.

A few days later I reached the end of the comics. I was sorry to see the stack end, because where would I get more reading material of the non-senior-citizen variety? The school library had books, but you couldn't check them out, and they looked even mustier than the comic books.

The box of comics was sitting on another cardboard box, which was filled with papers. It contained my mom's old report cards, mostly A's, some papers from a Jewish youth group, and other boring stuff, probably whatever was left over from my mom's old room when it became a laundry-folding and bill-paying room. I almost put the box away, but a brown piece of cardboard caught my attention.

I pulled it out and realized it was some kind of scrapbook. The cover said "1968" and "Susan Lowenstein," my mom's maiden name. Inside newspaper articles were taped to black pages with Scotch tape that was turning yellow and losing its stick. This scrapbook looked nothing like the ones my sister and her friends had made about their senior year, all girly stickers and funny-shaped scissors and things. This scrapbook was filled with newspaper articles, and most of them were not pleasant.

The articles were about civil rights protests on college campuses, protests that seemed to end with people getting hurt, jailed, or both. There were articles about Martin Luther King, Jr., but not about the speeches we heard in social studies — most were about him getting shot. Near the end of the scrapbook were some articles about riots: pictures of people looting stores, and policemen teargassing a crowd, and stories describing a city going crazy. At first I wasn't sure what city, but one caption mentioned Georgia Avenue and I knew it was here in D.C.

That night I tried to practice scales on the oboe, but I kept thinking about the pictures in the scrapbook, which I had stashed under the bed, and about Daron's warning to be careful about Diego. Those thoughts mixed together with my questions about what I was doing here, in my dead uncle's old bedroom, in Washington, D.C. The oboe squeaked, and I tried to focus on the notes, but it was useless. The more I played, the more distracted I became. I finally put the oboe out of its misery when I heard the phone ringing downstairs.

"Nine forty-five," I heard my grandfather say. "Who makes phone calls at nine forty-five at night?"

"Probably a telemarketer," said my grandmother.

Back in Maple Heights, my friend Josh and I used to have crazy conversations with telemarketers, until we got in trouble for scaring away Josh's mother's gynecologist.

The remote control didn't have a "mute" button, so the TV was turned off and I heard chairs creaking as both of my grandparents got up to answer.

Two more rings, and then my grandmother saying, "Hello?" in a worried voice. Then:

"Oh, hello, Mark," more coolly, more formal. "Yes, hold on please, I'll get him."

My dad. Of course, that was who would call at nine forty-five on Sunday night.

I heard my grandmother set the phone down on the kitchen table and then shuffle to the bottom of the stairs.

"Ethan!" she called. "Ethan, can you hear me? Your father's on the phone."

I put the oboe down on the bed. I hadn't talked to my dad in two months, since he had packed his stuff and moved out. If he wanted to talk to me so much, why didn't we both move back home and he could talk to me all he wanted?

"Ethan!" my grandmother called again.

If I picked up the phone, what would we talk about? I tried to remember other times I had talked to my dad without my sister moving the conversation along, or at least without the TV to distract us. I couldn't remember many times like that. And I didn't need to start now.

"I'm practicing!" I called downstairs.

I heard my grandmother sigh and shuffle back to the kitchen. She was talking more quietly now, but I heard her say "oboe" and then repeat, "Yes, he's playing the oboe now." After they hung up, I wondered if my grandmother would lecture me about how I really ought to talk to my dad. But when nobody came up the stairs, I went back to playing the oboe.

Later that night, I heard my grandparents talking in

their room. My grandmother was saying, "Remember when she was sick and he drove to her dorm with chicken soup?" And my grandfather said, "Hmmph. Sloshed all over the seats, and the car smelled like that soup as long as he had it." Then my grandmother turned on the faucet, so I didn't hear the rest of what they said.

When I heard "dorm," I assumed they were talking about Margo, but then I realized that she hadn't been in college long enough for anyone to drive to see her with chicken soup. Could they have been talking about my parents?

If there was anyone it was hard to imagine bringing chicken soup to a sick girl, it was my dad.

<<<　　>>>

Monday morning, Felix and Daron were waiting for me outside.

"Hey," said Felix, as I ran down the steps. "Did you get in trouble Friday? I wanted to come over but my dad made me mind my own business."

"No, but my grandmother said Mr. Harper has to call her before I can stay after school and practice anymore."

Felix nodded.

"My dad makes all kinds of people call him, too."

"Hey, Daron," I said, unable to control the next words

that came out of my mouth. "What did you mean when you said to be careful around Diego?"

He looked at me a minute.

"Nothing."

"He's just like that because of what happened to our mom," Felix said.

"What happened?" I said. I knew it was none of my business, but Felix had mentioned his mom twice now. He was practically begging me to ask.

"Your grandparents didn't tell you?" Felix said, sounding surprised. "It used to be all everybody said was" — he made his voice high and squeaky — "There go those poor Taylor boys. Ain't it a cryin' shame what happened to their mother? And that poor little baby girl! Mm-mm-mm, a cryin' shame.'"

Felix paused.

"Well, I guess mostly it was old ladies at church who did that," he said. "Your grandma don't really talk that way."

"I guess not," I said. Daron kicked a rock, and it skipped along the sidewalk in a perfectly straight line.

"So I figured you knew," said Felix. "She got shot."

"For real?" I didn't know what to say next. *I'm sorry? That sucks?* So I waited for Felix to continue.

"Now don't *you* go starting a 'poor Taylor boys' speech

53

on me," Felix said. "Do you want to hear what happened or not?"

"Sure," I said. "I mean, if you want to tell me."

Felix glanced at Daron, who had found another stone to kick.

"It's not like everybody else don't already know," he explained. He turned back to me.

"She was a night nurse at D.C. General before they got shut down. She had to take two buses both ways, and sometimes she had to wait a long time for the second bus. So this one time, while she was waiting, she went into Georgia Avenue Mini Mart to buy some butter pecan ice cream. That was her favorite kind. I like chocolate, Daron likes peanut butter, our dad likes fudge ripple, and Kameka likes strawberry, but she didn't like strawberry then 'cause she was just a baby."

We crossed Pennington Avenue, a block from school. I felt my feet slowing down so I could hear the rest of Felix's story. Daron had stopped kicking pebbles but he was still looking at the ground. Felix started talking faster.

"So our mom was coming out with her butter pecan ice cream when she got shot. This guy in a car was aiming for this other guy, and the other guy ran in the Mini Mart just when our mom was coming out."

It was quiet for a minute. I could hear kids waiting to

get into school, but they sounded far away, like I was listening through earplugs.

Daron's voice broke the tension.

"Felix, it ain't like she dead. Felix always skips the last part and leaves people thinking she dead."

"She might as well be," Felix said under his breath.

"You better not say that again. If she ever heard you say that — "

"She ain't going to," said Felix. He turned to me. "She lives in this place up in Maryland that's like a nursing home, only you don't have to be old to go there."

"She got her spine damaged," Daron explained.

"Yeah," said Felix. "So now she can't talk or move around or nothing, and most of the time she don't even act like she know you're there. Our dad takes us to see her every other Sunday, and our aunt takes us the other Sundays. The reason is, somebody's gotta stay home with Kameka, 'cause they won't let you in until you're eight years old. I was eight when my mom first went there, but at first they didn't believe that I was old enough and my dad had to bring in my birth certificate."

"Wow," I said, because I didn't know what else to say. We were outside the school by then, standing with everyone else waiting to be let in.

"That's just for now, though," said Felix. "Someday

55

we're going to move to Maryland so it's not such a big trip to see her. Why were we talking about this, again?"

"You were telling me why Daron doesn't like Spanish kids," I said.

"Oh yeah. Well, the kid who ran in the Mini Mart, he was Spanish, so we thought the guy with the gun might be Spanish too, but they never caught him. But ever since then Daron's been not so crazy about Spanish people."

Daron shook his head. "That ain't got nothing to do with it."

The crowd of kids squeezed us toward the door.

"Thanks for telling me," I said. I knew I should say more but I didn't know what. It was like my vocabulary was shrinking with each new piece of information. I couldn't wrap my brain around the fact that something so awful could happen to Felix and Daron's family, a normal family that raked leaves and stuff.

Sharita wasn't by our lockers, which was okay because it took me four tries to get mine open. She wasn't in first period either. Diego was in front of me, and when I sat down he smiled.

"Hey, E-man, how's it going?"

"Good," I said. In the back of my mind, I remembered Daron's warning. "How's it going with you?"

"Okay," he said. "Hey, who were those kids you were with before school?"

"My neighbors."

"The big one name Daron?"

"Yeah."

He looked like he was thinking about saying something else, but changed his mind when the teacher started talking.

After class, I wanted to ask him more, but in the hall he was talking in Spanish and laughing with Johnny and José. Sharita still hadn't come to school. She was absent a lot, I realized. She was the only other person I knew in eighth grade, so after class I walked around the halls reading flyers about yearbook sales, a "stay in school" poster contest, and tryouts for the step club. I got to second period just in time.

I ate my lunch on the stairs again: hardboiled eggs, celery sticks, and unsalted pretzels. But there were plenty of pretzels and I was too hungry to care that they were unsalted. It was an okay day. I had the sad news about Mrs. Taylor to think about, but no one had untucked my shirt, called me an albino, or falsely accused me of farting.

After school, I went to Mr. Harper's room.

"Here for your oboe lesson?" he said.

"Uh . . . my grandmother said you have to call her."

"And what shall I call her?" he asked. I didn't know how to answer his joke, so he laughed and said, "That will be fine. Would you write her phone number down for me? You can come with me to the office if you'd like . . . in case it takes two of us to convince her," he added.

"Okay."

I followed him down the hall into the main office, and we went into a little room with a telephone, a computer, and TV screens connected to the security cameras around school.

If Maple Heights Middle School had security cameras, everyone would have known that I wasn't the only one there that day after school. Josh and Caleb and Tyler would be on tape too. If Maple Heights Middle School had security cameras, I'd probably still be there, hanging out with my friends and getting on with my life.

While Mr. Harper dialed, I listened to the vice principal on the phone.

"I understand child care is an issue," she was saying, "but it's not my issue. My issue is that your daughter has been absent from school at least once every week this school year."

"Hello, Mrs. Oppenheimer?" Mr. Harper said, interrupting my eavesdropping. "Oh, I'm sorry, Mrs. Lowenstein." I hadn't told him my grandparents were my mother's parents, so of course their last name was different. "This is Mr. Paul Harper, the music instructor at Parker Junior High School."

Pause.

"Oh, he did? Good. Well, he's certainly a promising young musician, and I would say so even if he weren't standing next to me."

He laughed. Another pause.

"Four o'clock? Absolutely. I'll boot him out of my room promptly at four." He laughed again.

"Yes, you too, Mrs. Lowenstein. Goodbye, then."

He hung up the phone and turned to me.

"Well, that's good news. Your grandmother has ensured you won't have to deal with my musician's temper a moment past four o'clock. So we've got a lot of work to do in the next — " he checked his watch — "thirty-three minutes."

As we turned to leave, I heard Ms. Jarvis say, "Well, the next time you need a babysitter on a school day, I hope you remember you are responsible for *all* the children in your family. And that includes Sharita."

The Sharita I knew? How many Sharitas could there be at Parker? Who were absent on the same day? But she wouldn't have stayed home to babysit. Wasn't that against the law or something?

During the lesson, I kept thinking of things I could say to Sharita the next day: "Where were you yesterday?" "I missed you yesterday," "Please don't laugh because I noticed you were gone." I had forgotten the fingering I practiced over the weekend, and Mr. Harper had to show me the same things three or four times before they made sense.

But he just nodded whenever the oboe squeaked, like I was playing regular music.

6

After my lesson, I saw Diego shooting hoops in the school parking lot.

"There's my man, E-man," he called out.

"What, were you waiting for me?"

"Hey, it's an honor to get waited for by Diego. We wouldn't want you getting lost in your new neighborhood."

"Gee, thanks."

As we walked up Ninth Street, he asked, "So what do you do in there for jazz band?"

"We play music and stuff. We practice different parts where certain instruments have a hard time."

"How'd you learn to play clarinet anyway?"

I forgot I had told him what instrument I really played.

"We had to pick in fourth grade. I wasn't allowed to play drums, and I thought violins were for girls, so I picked clarinet."

"You picked lucky," he said. "Kids in jazz band always get into Ellington Arts for high school, and kids from Ellington always go to college. I want to go to college. Get me a hoodie sweatshirt with the name of my school, and then come back here and be like, make way for Diego the college man."

"You can go to college without being in jazz band."

"Maybe. But it don't usually work out like that."

"My sister Margo's in college," I said, "and she stopped playing the violin after seventh grade."

"Yeah," said Diego, "but she didn't go to no Garfield High School neither."

"Yeah," I said. I wouldn't go there either, would I?

"I got two brothers finished there. Well, one finished and one decided he was finished, you know. But neither of them can find a job for more than about two months. And it ain't looking better for my brother who's still there."

"Yeah," I said. "Well, then maybe you should join band."

Diego shook his head.

"It's too late," he said. "You gotta already know an instrument, 'cause Mr. Harper don't have time to be teaching kids from scratch."

I wanted to say he had time to teach me the oboe, but we had gotten to Tillerman Avenue and Diego was already saying goodbye. After I turned down the street, I looked over my shoulder and saw Diego quickly look around before hurrying on in the direction we were walking.

"How was the oboe lesson?" my grandmother asked when I walked in.

"Good."

"You got some more mail," my grandfather said, handing me a white envelope addressed in purple marker. Inside was a piece of green notebook paper.

October 16

Ethan-bequeathin',

Tell me when you get your email hooked up so I can stop with this archaic form of communication. How are you? Have you been calling Mom? She needs us now, even if it's hard to believe. Do you think they're going to split up for good?

Have you met any fun kids in D.C.? No offense, but I always thought your friends at home were a little twerpish. And in case you're wondering, I totally blame them for what happened to you.

Tutoring is OK. My friend Emma was going to do it with me, but her mom freaked out about her being in a "bad neighborhood." (Emma says that's not why she dropped out, but whatever.) Meanwhile, Mom has no idea I'm even doing this tutoring thing but I guess she sent you to live in a worse neighborhood anyway.

Well, I better go — class is starting. Midterms next week. Blah! Hope you like your new school and are having fun in D.C. Say hi to Grandma and Grandpa.

xoxo

Margo Pargo

I read the letter twice, standing in the kitchen. All I wanted was news from home, some hint that my friends and family remembered me. And what did I get from Margo? My friends are twerps, and Mom needs us. Yeah, right. Mom was the one who had practically forced my grandparents to keep me here. She thought I was so terrible after what happened, and she was embarrassed to be seen with me. Margo was so damn cheerful out in California. She liked to think she knew everything, but she didn't. Did I think our parents were going to split up? Just reading the question made me nauseous.

I looked up. My grandfather was reading a camping gear catalog, and my grandmother was putting a pan of chicken and mushy carrots in the oven. Old-people food looked a lot like baby food, I realized.

"How's your sister?" my grandmother asked.

"She says 'hi.'"

"How's she doing at school?"

"Fine."

"Has she picked a major yet?"

"I don't know." What was this, a trial? On the edge of the envelope, I practiced oboe fingering to give my hands something to do.

"Young people today have so many choices," she said. "Things our generation hadn't even heard of!"

"She said I should call Mom."

"What — does she have stock in the phone company?" my grandfather asked.

I smiled, thinking he was joking, but he didn't smile back.

"The whole time I was in the army," he said, "for nineteen months, I made exactly one long-distance call home, to tell my parents that I got my appendix out. The rest of the time, you know what I did?"

"Uh-uh."

"I called person-to-person. Back in those days, you could ask the operator to connect you to a specific person on the other end. So I'd make a person-to-person call to myself, and my mother would say I wasn't there. Then she'd hang up and know I was safe, and it didn't cost a penny."

"Do they still have person-to-person calling?" my

grandmother asked. "That's an expression I haven't heard in such a long time."

"Do I look like the phone company?" my grandfather said. "All I'm saying is what we used to do instead of spending money on long-distance calls."

"Well, you can't ask Ethan to make a person-to-person call if they don't have it anymore. And besides, if they didn't set it up ahead of time, Susan wouldn't know what to think, getting a person-to-person call for her son. You and your mother must have set it up ahead of time."

"I'm not saying he should call person-to-person," said my grandfather. "I'm just saying if you use your head, you can find a way to do the same thing for less. You don't see Margo calling long-distance every time she thinks of something to say. She picks up a pen and writes a letter."

"Actually," I said, "she wanted to send me email, but she didn't know if I could check it down here."

"I don't think I'll ever figure out how they get those computers to talk to each other," my grandmother said. "Do you know how that works, Ethan?"

"Well, I don't really know how it works, but it's easy to do. At home I email my friends all the time, and Margo, and, like, my teachers about homework and stuff."

"Hmmph," my grandfather said, returning to his catalog. "One minute it took to make a person-to-person call. And it didn't cost a penny."

My grandmother turned the temperature up for the chicken.

"Just because you don't hear on the phone doesn't mean no one else should pick the thing up, Ira. Ethan, go ahead and call after supper. Just wait until after seven when the rates go down."

After supper it was only five forty-five. Why did old people have to eat so early? To pass the time, I did my homework and reviewed the oboe music Mr. Harper had transcribed. At 7:03, I picked up the phone in the upstairs hallway. My mom answered after the first ring.

"Hello?"

"Hi, it's me."

"Ethan!" she said. "Hold on, let me get rid of my book club person on call waiting."

When she came back, I said, "Grandma and Grandpa are kind of freaked out about the phone bill, so I probably shouldn't talk long."

"Oh," she said. There was a pause, and I thought she might offer to call back. Instead she said, "It's okay. I've got a boatload of work tonight anyway."

"Oh, okay." It felt silly, what Margo said, that Mom needed checking up on.

"So, how are you? How's school?"

"Good," I said. I didn't mention eating lunch on the stairs or how most of the kids still looked at me like I was

66

from another planet. "I'm learning to play oboe in the jazz band."

"Oboe?" my mom said. "Wow, that's . . . wow."

I remembered my grandmother telling my dad, "Yes, he's playing the oboe now." I guess it wasn't every parent's dream to have their kid be the world's first jazz oboist.

"And the kids there . . . ?"

"They're okay," I said. "I've been walking to school with the kids next door, Felix and Daron."

I didn't mention Diego because I didn't think I could summarize him in a phone conversation. I definitely didn't mention Sharita. And I didn't mention the seven hundred other kids at school. I twisted the phone cord around and around my hand.

"Oh, I remember the Taylor boys," my mom said. "And their poor mother, is she still hanging on?"

Felix was right: after something bad happens to you, it's always the first thing everyone thinks of.

"Yeah, she's still alive. They visit her on Sundays."

"Mm-mm-mm," my mom said. "And Grandma and Grandpa, how are they?"

"Good," I said. There was a pause. "Do you want to say hi to them?"

"I'd love to," my mom said, "but I'm on my way out the door."

"Okay. Bye."

Whatever I had expected from the phone call, that wasn't it. My grandfather was right; it wasn't worth the five cents a minute or whatever it had cost.

And it was beginning to make sense that my grandparents didn't visit us in Maple Heights. Either my grandfather would have to drive two and a half hours there and two and a half hours back, or else they'd have to pay for train tickets. Then they'd have to pay more money for a hotel, or else stay in our house, where people slept different hours and ate different food than they were used to. It was stupid, but I could see how these things kept them from visiting us.

Why we didn't visit them was more of a mystery. When Margo and I would ask, my mom always said, "Your grandparents don't live in a nice part of the city. There isn't much space there for kids to play." That never seemed like the whole story. And now that I was living here, it made even less sense. Only Margo was good about staying in touch with them, sending little cards and notes — just like she was sending me now. It could drive a person crazy, the chatty little notes that didn't tell me anything I wanted to know. I was sick of my family's easy answers and their generic greeting-card approach to life. For once, I wanted to know what was real.

7

The next morning I realized that both pairs of my navy blue pants and long-sleeve dress shirts were dirty. I put on one of the short-sleeve shirts and the pants from the day before, which were crumpled up on the closet floor.

"I hope you're not thinking of leaving the house like that," my grandmother said when I sat down for breakfast.

"Like what?"

"Like a hoodlum who doesn't know how to take care of his clothes," she snapped. "If you want to freeze in your shirt-sleeves, fine, but you're not going out with wrinkled pants. You'll find the iron in the hall closet upstairs."

It took a long time to get the iron down, because there were about a hundred towels and a hair dryer crammed in the shelf around it. Also, I didn't know how to iron. I was standing at the bathroom sink in my shirt and underwear waiting for the iron to heat up when I caught a glimpse of my grandfather in the doorway, smiling.

"Your grandmother making you do that?"

"Yeah."

He opened the hall closet and handed me the hair dryer. The lady on the box had wide, feathered hair.

"This is almost as good, and you can keep your pants on."

"Really?"

I spent a few minutes blow-drying my pants, but they only looked slightly neater and my knees were getting hot. Oh, well. It was time to go.

When I came downstairs for the second time, my grandmother shook her head at me.

"Did your grandfather have you blow-dry those?"

"Uhh . . ."

"I could hear the hair dryer down here," she said, handing me two pieces of toast with margarine. "Here, eat this while you walk to school."

I knew I'd be starving by second period. I missed frozen chocolate-chip waffles more than I would have thought possible.

It was cold, but the bright sunlight hurt my eyes. When Felix saw the toast, he smirked.

"Ooh, did you sleep late and miss breakfast? That happens to Daron all the time, don't it, Daron? I like to get up early, but Daron could sleep and sleep all day if you let him. He don't get tired at night, though. Sometimes I wonder if he ever even go to sleep."

Daron's eyes narrowed and he looked at his brother sideways.

Felix shrugged.

"I can't help it. If you share a room with somebody, you notice what time they go to sleep at night. And some nights, like last night, I don't think he lay down in his bed more than five minutes in a row. 11:37, I wake up 'cause Daron's making noise over on his side of the room. 12:08, I wake up 'cause Daron's going out of our room. 2:19, I wake up 'cause Daron's coming into our room. In and out all night, it's amazing I can wake up for school."

Felix paused for a moment. "Hey, Daron, where do you go all night anyway?"

"I got insomnia." He looked at Felix and added, "That means I don't sleep good."

"I know that word," Felix said. "I-N-S-O-M-N-I-A. But where do you go when you got your insomnia?"

Daron's voice was steady. "Wander around the house. Sometimes I watch TV without the sound and make up my own words to them info-mercials."

"For real?" Felix said. "Maybe one night I'll stay up late and make 'em up with you."

"They're not about stuff you like," said Daron.

Felix shrugged and scrunched up his nose, trying to wiggle his ears.

‹‹‹   ›››

Sharita was back at school, wearing one yellow sock and one green sock, with shiny stuff on her lips. When lunchtime came, I was ready for her, even though I had spent most of third period wishing for chocolate-chip waffles. When Sharita got to her locker, I had finished jiggling the lock on mine and put my grandmother's plastic-bag lunch in my backpack. I then stood casually with the locker door open so it wouldn't look like I was waiting for her.

While she turned the numbers on her lock, I closed my locker door and said, "Hi."

She jumped about three feet in the air, so my subtle locker-door closing must have been louder than I thought. But she smiled and said "hi" back. Then she returned to turning numbers on her lock.

"How was yesterday?" I said.

She looked at me suspiciously.

"Fine."

"Were you sick?" I blurted. I didn't tell her what I had overheard.

"No, my nephew was." Then her face brightened. "Want to see his picture?"

"Sure." I would have looked at the insides of an

orangutan if it meant she would stand in the hall and talk to me.

Lockers slammed, and somebody pushed up against me from behind. Sharita unzipped her purple pocketbook and pulled out a matching wallet that had space for about ten pictures. She started at the beginning.

"That's my cousin last year at her graduation. That's my sister, and that's my other sister, and that's my friend Monique who moved away. That's my brother, and that's my grandma, and that's my mom when she was young. Okay, ready?"

"Uh huh." I was ready for anything.

She flipped the page so I could see the photo on the left.

"That's Jamil."

Jamil was wearing blue overalls with a red train on the front. He looked like he was about Kameka's age.

"Cute," I said.

"And this," she said, uncovering the other picture, "is Latasha."

Latasha was a little baby, curled up in a pink blanket.

"Awwww," I said, and I meant it.

"She's five months old," Sharita said, "and Jamil is three and a half."

"And he was sick yesterday?"

"Yeah. Just a little fever, but his daycare place won't let

him in with a fever. And my sister just started this new job, so she couldn't take off."

"So you had to watch him?"

"You think I can't keep up with school?" she said. "I don't need this from you on top of everybody else."

"No, I — you just shouldn't have to miss school like that."

Sharita shrugged. "It's better than being here. And I get a lot more free time when I don't have to ride three buses each way. Yesterday at home I read half of *Great Expectations* and we made brownies."

"Did you bring any?"

Sharita rolled her eyes.

"No. My sister's boyfriend came over with two of his friends, so those brownies lasted maybe five minutes. It's good I let Jamil have one before dinner or he wouldn't have even gotten one."

"You're a good aunt," I said.

"Yeah?"

"Yeah."

We walked to the cafeteria together, and it felt like the most natural thing in the world. I even wondered if we might eat lunch together, but of course she got in line for hot food. Like every normal kid at this school.

"Well, see ya, Ethan."

"Yeah. See ya."

74

I waited for Sharita to turn around so she wouldn't see me sneak out of the cafeteria to eat lunch on the stairs (which I had gone back to doing after the only teacher who cared about it had quit). But as I headed for the side door, I heard someone call "E-man!"

Diego was motioning me over to his table. José and Johnny were smiling at me, but not in a friendly way.

"Sit down," Diego said, and for some stupid reason I listened.

I sat between Diego and Johnny. What did they want? I hoped they didn't notice my lunch: carrot sticks, oatmeal cookies, store-brand ginger ale, plus a turkey sandwich on rye bread and some applesauce in an old margarine container.

"You're late," Diego said. "What, did ya get lost?"

"I was talking to somebody." *Dumb.* They must have seen me walk in with Sharita, and I didn't have to make it a big deal.

"Sharrrita!" said Johnny. He rolled his "r" to make it sound like she was a Spanish señorita wearing a flamenco dancing costume.

Diego yelled, "I win the bet, I win the bet, you owe me, José! You owe me big time!"

"No, you said the first girl he get it on with, not the first girl he walk in the cafeteria with," said José.

Diego said, "No, we just said the first girl he *be* with.

75

You said Spanish and I said black. But where you think the two of them been the last fifteen minutes? I might've won either way."

Diego shrugged.

"I had better odds. I mean, look around this school. But I thought you'd at least wait 'til, I don't know, maybe the weekend?"

The three of them burst out laughing until Johnny choked on the soda in his mouth. I wanted to crawl under the table.

"Where'd you do it?" he asked after he got his breath back. "The janitor's closet?"

"The A.V. room?" said Diego.

"The book room?"

Even in Maple Heights, where I hung around the popular kids, no one would have thought I was cool enough to have sex with a girl. But listening to them talk about Sharita like that didn't make me feel cool.

"We were just talking, okay?" I said. Then I added, "When I give it to a woman, I make it last more than fifteen minutes."

"All right!" Diego said and high-fived me.

Johnny couldn't stop laughing.

"That's good," he said, "that's real good. When I give it to a woman I make it take a long time too."

José nodded slowly and grinned.

"You got the right idea, with them girls from Southeast. They make it worth your while to leave the neighborhood."

I felt oatmeal cookies and rye bread churning around in my stomach. I shoved my grandmother's spoon and margarine container into the bottom of my backpack and bolted out of the cafeteria.

8

Felix was waiting for me outside the cafeteria.

"What are you doing here?" I asked, breathing hard to avoid puking.

He showed me his bathroom pass. "I gotta ask you something."

I could still see Diego, Johnny, and José in the cafeteria, and they weren't smiling. I moved a few steps away from the door, forcing Felix to follow me.

"What's wrong?" I asked. He was biting the insides of his cheeks.

"I gotta ask you, I mean, because you're my next door neighbor and everything. Even though you haven't been my next door neighbor long, it's not like you're a random person on the street, you know, 'cause you live on *my* street."

"Okay," I said. I must have known Felix better than I realized, because that actually made sense to me.

"Okay. Did Daron seem normal to you this morning? What he said about walking around at night, not sleeping?"

How would I know what was normal around here? Daron was a tall ninth-grader who acted like he knew what was going on.

"I don't know. I guess."

Felix's mouth stopped moving so rarely that when it happened, I took him seriously. "When Daron can't sleep, he's not walking around watching no TV," he said.

"What's he doing?"

"I don't know. But I keep waking up 'cause I hear the front door open, and we ain't got cable TV on the front steps."

"Doesn't your dad wake up?"

Felix shook his head.

"Our dad could sleep through a dump truck smashing into our living room. This one time, it was like, midnight, and me and Daron flushed Rice Krispies down the toilet to see if we could make them explode. We flooded the whole bathroom. Our dad slept through the whole thing and would've kept sleeping except I accidentally dripped water on him when I went to check if he was awake."

"So where do you think Daron is going at night?"

"I don't know, but you gotta help me find out. Can you

come over tomorrow night? Like around midnight? I'll try to find out more by then."

"Midnight?" My grandparents worried when I came home at four-thirty. Didn't Felix have a better friend than me, someone else he could ask to spy on his brother?

Felix sighed. "What time do your grandparents go to sleep?"

"Around ten most nights, I guess. My grandfather sometimes falls asleep in front of the TV and then goes to bed."

"So you could come over at midnight if you wanted to," Felix said. He was biting the insides of his cheeks again. His shirt had come untucked on one side and his tongue was the color of grape candy.

The hall was almost empty and I was late for class. "I don't know — I'll let you know. But I gotta go."

I ran up the stairs to social studies, but when I got there the door was locked. I jiggled the handle, thinking it got locked by mistake, and I saw a couple of kids laugh. Mr. Kirk came to the door.

"Have a little trouble getting here on time after lunch?" he asked.

"Sort of," I said. "My neighbor started — "

Mr. Kirk interrupted me. "If you arrive late to my class, you'll find that rattling the doorknob accomplishes nothing except perhaps getting you written up for disruption.

You will sit silently in this hallway, and when class is over you will find one of your classmates and ask very kindly if he or she will let you catch up on the work you missed."

Then the door clicked shut. Through the window, I could see a question scratched on the chalkboard: "Who and what shaped the civil rights movement?" Underneath was a list of bullet points with names and phrases: Martin Luther King, Jr.; Malcolm X; Rosa Parks; Jim Crow; *Plessy v. Ferguson; Brown v. Board of Education;* Little Rock High School; Sixteenth Street Baptist Church; Civil Rights Act; Fair Housing Act. Then there were three bullet points with question marks, like to say the list could go on. Some of the things I had heard of before, and some of them I hadn't.

I kicked the row of tile below the lockers, but that just reminded me how much my toes hurt in the penny loafers. I turned around and sat on the floor, near a couple of candy wrappers and a note someone had shredded into tiny pieces. The hall smelled like stale gum and gym sneakers.

From this angle, I saw scuff marks where kids had kicked their lockers, and different-colored gum stuck inside a big air vent at the end of the hall. I heard the hum of teachers' voices, a chair scraping against the floor, music coming from the Spanish classroom across the hall.

It wasn't fair. Mr. Kirk had turned on me, after being

on my side about the shirt untucking. I hoped he wouldn't call my grandparents. I didn't know what they would do to me, but I didn't want to find out.

I sat there for twenty minutes. I heard once that prisoners sometimes go crazy from boredom, and after they're released, they get locked up in a mental hospital. Could that happen to me? To be safe, I took out my oboe music. For the rest of the period, I held a pencil like an oboe, moving my fingers where the music said they should go.

When class ended, I had to hurry and put my pencil and sheet music away so I didn't get run over. Should I look happy I missed class, or try to get the work? My answer came out of the classroom wearing sparkly glasses and mismatched socks.

"Hi," Sharita said.

"Hi." I noticed the other kids noticing us, but I didn't care. Did they all think like José about girls from Southeast?

"I was late once on the first week of school, and it was about ninety-five degrees in this hallway," she said. "At least it's October now."

"I got to practice 'In the Mood' a little. I used a pencil like an oboe." *Dumb, Ethan, dumb.* A cool kid who was happy to get thrown out of class wouldn't sit in the hallway pretending to play an oboe.

Sharita laughed, and we started walking down the hall.

"I do that all the time. Once I was using my fork like a trombone, and I got spaghetti sauce all over my brother. Want to know what you missed in class?"

"Was it a lot?"

"That depends how important you think our civil rights project is. If you want to know your topic or your partner or whatever."

Partner? I was too new to think about partners. How would I find someone?

Sharita watched me worrying about the possibilities. "Don't have a heart attack. Mr. Kirk gave us partners."

Phew.

"Yeah, I know. It's better, but people still find a way, you know? Like, 'Ew! I'm not working with that girl! I had to work with her last time!'"

I could tell we weren't talking about my partner anymore.

"But you're the smartest person in the class," I said. "I mean, you read *Great Expectations* in one day. Wouldn't everyone want to be your partner and then just hope you do all the work? I mean, that's not — I mean, there's other reasons they'd want to be your partner too."

"Whatever. They don't think so."

"But — "

"If, like, you don't have a lot of money, or if you got people in your family made mistakes or whatever, they act

83

like it's contagious or something. Okay? Is that good enough for you?"

"Sorry, I — "

"Whatever. Do you want to know who your partner is?"

"Yeah."

"It's Diego."

"Diego?"

"Yeah, he just kind of shrugged when he found out. It shouldn't be too bad. I don't know if he'll do any work, though."

I wanted to ask her where Southeast was, and about her family, and what kind of music she liked, but we had reached the band room. Mr. Harper was standing in the door, waving his arms.

"Come on, come on!" he was saying to everyone who walked in. "Time is passing us by! We need to get all the way through 'In the Mood' if we're to even think of moving on to our new piece today. And what a new piece it is! Let's go, ladies and gentlemen, let's go!"

I couldn't say anything to Sharita in the chaos of everyone grabbing instruments, but while we were warming up I watched her smooth leg, the one with the yellow sock, tap a secret rhythm on the floor.

We sounded pretty good. Even I sounded less awful than I had a few weeks ago. With five minutes left in the class period, Mr. Harper held up a stack of brand-new sheet music from his podium at the front of the room.

"I hope you all enjoy this music as much as I do. And if you do, you can demonstrate that by not folding, bending, rumpling, eating near, or spitting on this brand-new sheet music we were fortunate enough to have donated to us this year. Are there any questions?"

"Yeah," said Anthony, from the end of my row. His trumpet reflected the fluorescent lights in the ceiling. "What song is it?"

A few kids laughed, and Mr. Harper looked at the stack of sheet music still in his hand.

"An excellent question, Mr. Lomax, an excellent question." He handed the music to the first kid in each row, and everyone took one and passed the rest down.

"A classic jazz tune for the holidays: 'Boogie Woogie Santa Claus.'"

"Hey, he said 'booger,'" said Anthony.

"Shut up," someone else said, "That's a cool song."

"I love that song!" I heard Sharita say.

Mr. Harper removed a piece of blank paper that was taped to the board. I was surprised to see my name listed as one of six kids with a solo in this piece.

"I'll have the oboe part transcribed for you tomorrow," Mr. Harper said to me.

"Thanks," I mumbled.

It figured. Christmas music. What did I expect for a December concert? In case I wasn't different enough, having to get my music specially transcribed, the world's only jazz oboist also happened to be Jewish. I had never decorated a Christmas tree, never hung a Christmas stocking, and definitely never had Santa Claus boogie-woogie down my chimney.

If I was never going to fit in, why bother trying? That thought was enough to make me decide to do the craziest thing I could think of: sneak out with Felix to spy on his brother.

9

Cooped up in my grandparents' house, eating old-people food and having only my oboe for company, I needed a plan to improve my social life. Maybe helping Felix could even be the first step. I thought about it during my oboe lesson, wondering if I could really sneak out without getting in trouble.

"Mr. Oppenheimer!" Mr. Harper sounded alarmed. "Didn't you notice those two pages of music stuck together? You skipped over your solo."

"Oh. Sorry." I turned back to the page I had skipped, but Mr. Harper put his hand in front of the music.

"Mr. Oppenheimer," he said, "it's fine and good for music to be a mirror into your soul. But put too many mirrors together, you end up with a fun house. And that's not very musical at all."

I wasn't sure exactly what he meant, but I liked the part about music being a mirror into my soul.

He looked at his watch. "Although it is six minutes until four, my impression is that you might need those six minutes to keep from stepping off the curb in front of a truck. Be careful on your way home."

I smiled. Things were looking up now that I had decided to help Felix. I grabbed my backpack, coat, and Phillies cap, and headed outside.

I was wearing the hat because that morning my grandmother had insisted I cover my head. She wanted me to wear one of my grandfather's hats, but no way was I putting one of those smelly gray wool things on my head. "I have my own," I told her, shoving my Phillies cap into my backpack before she could study it closely. When my dad bought it for me at my first baseball game, I had to tilt it all the way back on my head so it didn't cover my eyes. Now it fit just right.

Outside, it was quiet. It was even too cold for anyone to be standing in front of Georgia Avenue Liquors. I was about halfway home when two guys appeared, stepping out right in front of me. One of them was husky, and the other one was more athletic-looking, but both looked like they could beat me up without a problem. They had navy blue bandannas on their heads, and it took me a second to recognize who they were without the school uniforms: Diego's friends from the cafeteria.

"Nice hat," José said, not smiling.

I moved a couple of steps to the right, closer to the houses, but Johnny and José got in front of me again. They didn't seem like people to reason with. Could anything in my backpack — what? Hurt them? Distract them? And how would I take off my backpack without them grabbing it? My oboe — Mr. Harper's oboe — was in there.

"Leave him alone!" called a voice from Singleton Avenue.

I didn't see anyone, but in a few seconds Diego appeared.

"Hey, leave him alone, he don't know, man." He said something in Spanish and then turned to me. "Tell them you're wearing the hat because you like the Phillies."

That was close enough. "Yeah, I'm from Philadelphia. That's my home team."

They didn't look convinced. I didn't seem like someone "from Philadelphia," even to myself. José said something in Spanish, and Diego interrupted. I didn't understand what he said, but I heard the word "gringo," which I knew meant me.

Johnny looked at José and shrugged.

"Okay, kid, we take Diego's word for it. But a little fashion advice — " And José grabbed my Phillies cap before I could even react. "Leave the hat home," and he threw it back to me.

Johnny and José disappeared as quickly as they had arrived, and I was left lamely holding my hat in my hand. Diego shifted his weight from one side to the other.

"Sorry about them," he said. "They get what you might call a little over-enthusiastic."

"Because of my hat?"

"There's certain blocks where you don't wear certain colors. Like Columbia Heights? I wouldn't *ever* wear that hat in Columbia Heights."

I nodded like I knew where Columbia Heights was, like I went there all the time.

"Gangs?" I guessed.

"Yeah. But it's not that bad. It just sounds bad when you explain it."

"Okay."

"I guess you don't have gangs in Maple Syrup-ville, huh?"

"Maple — " He had messed up the name on purpose, to tease me. "No, not too many."

"I never been to Pennsylvania before. Someday I want to visit all fifty states."

"How many are you up to?"

"Three," he said, "counting D.C., so my total is out of fifty-one. So far I've been to D.C. and Maryland, and I went to Virginia once on a trip."

I thought about my friends in Maple Heights who

went skiing in Vermont or Colorado every winter and vacationed in places like California in the summer.

"You might not like Pennsylvania. There's not much to do in Maple Heights."

"That sounds pretty good to me."

There was a pause.

Then Diego said, "We're gonna be partners in social studies. For that civil rights project or whatever."

"Yeah, I heard." Another pause. "I'm sorry I missed the day we got the information. I, uh, I heard we have to turn in an outline next week."

"Okay."

"Do we have to . . . go to the library or something?" I said.

"Yeah. Can you go Saturday? I could go at, like, three."

"Okay. Uh, where's the library?"

"Newbie." He smiled. "E-man, can I call you Newbie? Okay, Newbie, what you do is, take the 42 bus down Georgia Avenue until it goes over to Seventh Street. Then you get off at Seventh and G and walk to Ninth and G. That's the Martin Luther King Library."

"Okay. I'll check and let you know tomorrow." I hoped Diego didn't find out I had never been on a bus, other than a school bus, before. "Uh, one more thing? What's our topic?"

Diego smiled again, but this time it was more of a devilish grin. He made his fingers into claws so he looked a little like a tiger when he shouted, "Riots!"

‹‹‹   ›››

Dinner was chicken again, a little dried out, with baked potatoes and mushy carrots. After the meal, my grandfather stood up for the six o'clock news. I decided it was as good a time as any to bring up the subject of me going to the library. They didn't mind me walking to school with Felix and Daron, I reasoned, so why would they mind if I met Diego at the library? Hopefully I could change the topic if they asked where Diego lived, or who his parents were, or anything else about him.

As my grandparents settled down in front of the TV, I said, "I have this project to work on for social studies. We're learning about civil rights."

"I remember in school we always used to learn about the Indians before Thanksgiving," my grandmother said.

"I don't think this is for Thanksgiving."

"Hmm," said my grandfather. "What have you learned so far?"

"We're just starting. And we're meeting Saturday at the Martin Luther King Library. There's a bus I can take down Georgia Avenue — "

"The whole class is going down Georgia Avenue on a bus?" my grandmother asked.

"No, just my group. It's the only time we can meet to do it."

"And who's in this group?" my grandmother wanted to know.

"Some kids from my class." That was true; two kids counted as "some." "I don't know the whole class's names yet." Also true.

My grandfather looked at the clock: 6:02. He had missed the beginning of the news.

"Surely you don't expect us to let you take a bus downtown to meet some kids whose names you don't even know," he said.

"I know the names of the people in my group. I just don't know the names of the whole class."

"In my day," said my grandfather, "that kind of answer would be called smart-mouth, and you wouldn't be going anywhere on Saturday."

"Sorry. It's Diego. The teacher assigned us a partner."

"Hmm," said my grandmother. "Well, I guess you have to go to the library, but you certainly don't have to get there on the bus. Your grandfather will take you after his retired pharmacists' breakfast."

She switched on the TV, and a perky announcer came on. "When we come back, our money doctor will look into the magic of compound interest."

"Hmmph," said my grandfather to the TV. "In my day,

people used to *work* for a living. None of this hocus pocus."

"What kind of breakfast?" I asked.

"There's a group of retired pharmacists that has breakfast once a month at Toojay's," my grandfather said. It was like he was challenging me not to laugh out loud.

"I didn't know you were a pharmacist," I said.

"Not just a pharmacist, I had my own store. Me and my cousin Jerry, on the corner of Fourteenth and R."

I imagined an old-fashioned drugstore with kids at the counter drinking milkshakes.

"Can we go there sometime?"

My grandfather waved his hand. "Nothing left of it," he said, and just then the news came back on.

"Are you paying too much for prescription drugs?" the commercial asked cheerfully, and my grandmother turned up the volume.

"I can at least take the bus home," I offered, louder than the TV.

My grandmother practically had to shout over the noise. "You most certainly cannot. Your grandfather will wait for you in the lobby, and then he'll drive you home."

Not exactly what I had hoped for, but at least I was getting out of the house on Saturday. And in just under thirty hours, I'd be leaving the house unnoticed, to help Felix spy on his brother.

10

Wednesday night I made a chart like one I had made for science in seventh grade, for observations about the moon. If anyone asked what I was doing outside in the middle of the night, I'd pull out the chart. "Moon-watching," I'd say.

Then I played the oboe for half an hour. My grandfather knocked on the door to tell me he was going to bed, but first he wanted to congratulate me on my medical breakthrough.

"Huh?" I said.

"My doctor was wrong — I don't need hearing aids after all! Your oboe playing has restored my damaged senses."

He hummed "Wonder of Wonders, Miracle of Miracles" from *Fiddler on the Roof* as he shuffled into the hallway.

I set my alarm for 11:55 and lay down on top of the brown blanket. My feet dangled off the edge of the bed. I noticed that my sneakers were tighter than when I first got here, and the blanket was worn and soft.

I tried to sleep, but I kept thinking about home, where my dad didn't live, and where my sister didn't live, and how I hadn't written back to her. And how my friends back home weren't really my friends, and how I probably had no chance in the world with the beautiful girl from jazz band. And how I was lying in a dead guy's bed, one with a weird, depressing scrapbook stashed beneath it. At 11:50 I turned off the alarm, then I slid off the bed and scooped the moon chart from the top of the dresser.

I tiptoed down the stairs one at a time, near the wall, where they didn't creak as much. My grandfather snored quietly. I left the door unlocked, hoping that no one would break into the house.

Then I stepped outside. The streetlights made our block look warm, but it was freezing. A breeze blew through the Taylors' big tree, the one that shed all the leaves.

How would I tell Felix I was there? In a movie, the main character would throw pebbles at the guy's window, but I didn't know which room was his. Plus, didn't he share a room with Daron? What if Daron was home and Felix had canceled the whole thing? Or worse, what if my grandparents heard? This was crazy. This was not the kind of thing anyone worried about in Maple Heights.

Then the Taylors' front door opened slightly, and a small body slipped through.

"You came!" Felix said, grinning. "Man, it's freezing! Didn't your grandparents buy you no coat?"

They hadn't, but my jacket from home was hanging in the closet six inches from the front door.

"I didn't think of it."

"I gotta think of everything!" Felix said, but he didn't sound mad. "Stay here."

He ran back to the house, his feet crunching a couple of stray leaves. He opened the door a crack, slipped in, slipped out, then ran back across the lawn and handed me a navy blue hoodie.

"Here. It's Daron's, so don't get it dirty."

"Thanks," I said, pulling it over my head.

Our street was asleep. I thought about Felix and Daron's mother, the night she got shot. Maybe some of the houses that looked asleep had people working the night shift. Either way, it was the most quiet I had ever experienced Washington.

"Come on, or we might miss him," Felix said.

"How do you know where he went?"

Felix smiled, like he was proud of his detective work.

"I heard him talking with one of his high school friends after school. He thought I went back inside for my math book, but then I remembered I had left it at home from

97

yesterday, and that's why I didn't have it. Did you know you can get a zero just for forgetting your book?"

"For real?"

"Yeah."

Our voices sounded far away, like they belonged to other people. I followed Felix to the corner, glancing back to make sure no lights had come on in my grandparents' house. They hadn't. I folded the moon chart and stuck it in a pocket. On Georgia Avenue, lights shone inside the All-Nite Pizza Deli and the police station. A car waited at the intersection, and zoomed ahead when the light turned green.

We turned left, and I realized we were taking the same route we walked every morning to school. Felix had stopped jabbering, and he led me around the side of a car with two flat front tires. The pavement was cool and smooth, and for a second I was back in Maple Heights, hiding behind a bush instead of a car. "Focus!" I heard Mr. Harper's voice say in my head.

"Where is he?" I whispered.

Felix put a finger in front of his lips.

Hiding made it feel like we were doing something wrong, even though we were trying to help Daron. We could hear cars whizzing by and the loud screeching of a bus, then a siren. After about ten minutes, we heard footsteps, and then voices:

" — the third time!"

"They think you stupid?"

"You don't pull that kind of — "

Another bus went by, so we missed what came next. The voices were just on the other side of the car. Were these gang members? Was Daron even here? I wondered what these guys would do to a couple of junior-high kids hiding behind an abandoned car.

"They be pulling that every time, 'Our supplier, see, he just didn't get it yet!'"

"You know you right about that."

"But Leon get hurt and don't nobody get nothin'."

"You gotta hurt somebody that don't matter."

Another car went by. Someone shouted out the window, and we heard glass break. Being here was starting to seem like a very bad idea.

" — that little guy I see them with."

"Daron could get him here."

Felix and I looked at each other. If we were in my uncle's comic books, we would have yelled for everyone to freeze, grabbed Daron, and zapped him right home. But Daron would learn how to shoot lightning bolts before he let two younger kids rescue him, even if Felix was his brother.

"Daron! I forgot you still in junior high!"

"You know the kid we mean?"

"I think so," said Daron.

"Little scruffy guy?"

"I think his name's Diego," said Daron.

"Daron the man!"

"Hey, Daron, you get him here tomorrow night."

"Get him here at midnight — "

"And you'll get promoted from junior associate."

"That'll be, like, the first time ever."

"We never had no regular member from junior high before."

"Okay," said Daron.

"You the man!"

"Hey, Daron, you walking up Georgia or Ninth?"

"Probably Ninth Street."

"Cool. That's how me and Tavon go."

"Don't scare no old ladies, the three of you walking like a bunch of thugs."

Some guys laughed. We heard a few "See ya's" and "Later's," and then the group split in different directions. Felix and I looked at each other. I still wasn't a hundred percent sure what was happening, but it was clear that we were stuck until everybody left. We sat with our backs against the car, like we were welded to it, like if the tires were magically fixed and someone got in the driver's seat, they could drive all the way to Union Station without noticing us. Then we could take the first train to somewhere else. Anywhere Daron didn't have to turn in Diego to get promoted.

A few minutes later, when I looked at Felix again, his lip was wobbling. We stood up and walked across the parking lot. As we turned right on Ninth Street I finally said, "Why do they want your brother to get Diego for them?"

Felix didn't laugh at me for not understanding, for being a dumb white kid from the suburbs.

"Diego's got a lot of brothers and cousins," he said. "They think if they hurt Diego, they can get what they want from those other guys."

"Oh." Our feet crunched some leaves on the sidewalk. "Do you think Daron will do it?"

"He always does what he says he'll do. Like one time he said he'd take me to an arcade on my birthday, only we got there and the arcade was closed. So we got on a bus all the way across the city to this other arcade. That was a great day."

"Yeah," I said, even though I wasn't there.

"Yeah."

Why had he brought me there? What would he do next? What was I supposed to do about Diego?

When we got back to our houses, Felix asked, "Do you think he's already inside?"

"I don't know where else he'd go."

Felix nodded.

"Me neither. Hey, don't forget the sweatshirt."

I pulled it over my head.

"Thanks for lending it to me."

"Thanks for coming."

I turned the doorknob gently and went inside. I tip-toed upstairs, walking close to the wall again, listening for my grandfather's snoring.

Then I got into bed and remembered I had left the stupid moon chart in the pocket of Daron's sweatshirt.

11

When my alarm went off the next morning, I was dreaming about being eaten alive by giant shrubbery, and the big brown blanket had gotten tangled around my legs. That kind of thing never happened with my comforter at home.

Felix barely said a word on the way to school, but if Daron noticed, he didn't comment. Daron didn't wander off with his friends right away, so I couldn't talk to Felix about getting rid of the moon chart.

During first period I was too distracted to pay attention to anything. I made two lists for myself: reasons to warn Diego (which I abbreviated R2WD) and reasons not to warn Diego (RN2WD). Under R2WD, I wrote:

These guys are scary, and Diego could get hurt.

But under RN2WD, I wrote:

These guys are scary — it would be smart for me to stay away from them.

Then, under R2WD:

Diego has been kind of a friend here (telling me about jazz band, convincing his friends my Phillies cap was just a hat, and being my partner in social studies).

But under RN2WD:

He hasn't been that much of a friend (I still eat lunch on the stairs because his friends are such a-holes to me, and he's only my partner because we were assigned).

Then, back to R2WD:

If Diego doesn't show up, maybe Daron would stop sneaking out at night.

But under RN2WD:

If Diego doesn't show up, maybe those guys would be mad at Daron, and who knows what would happen?

I was looking at my lists, trying to come up with another item for one side or the other, when Sharita walked in, five minutes late. She was wearing a royal blue V-neck shirt, and from the side I could see the exact shape of her left breast. If I put my elbow on the desk and leaned my face against my palm, I could watch the breast move while Sharita got out her pencil, notebook, and homework, and began the Mathercize warm-up.

Ms. Franklin went over the first two problems in the Mathercize and then stopped abruptly.

"Sharita, do you have a uniform pass?"

I didn't know what a uniform pass was, but I hoped she

had one. Maybe then she could always wear shirts like that.

"No," said Sharita. "Everything else was in the wash. My nephew — "

"You need a pass," Ms. Franklin interrupted.

Sharita sighed and pushed her chair back loudly before she left the room.

She came back ten minutes later, while Ms. Franklin was telling us what to study for a test next week. But she didn't stay. She grabbed her books and stared at Ms. Franklin for a couple of long seconds. Then she was gone again. A few kids laughed, the same way they laughed when Lyle falsely accused me of farting. I remembered what Sharita said about people judging her based on money and her family and whatever. But until then, I was so busy trying not to get laughed at myself that I didn't notice how people treated her.

I didn't see Sharita for the rest of the day.

I took good notes for her in our classes, the best notes I've ever taken. It took my mind off the Diego lists.

But the more I thought about it, the more the reasons to warn Diego were winning. If I were to tell him, how would I do it? And when? At lunchtime, my locker opened on the first try, which seemed like an omen. In the cafeteria, I sat down at Diego's table and waited.

And waited. Had Johnny and José seen me and sat

somewhere else? Waiting made me hungry, and I took a bite of my chicken salad sandwich. It was on a roll, which wasn't quite as old-people as rye bread. But what was that squooshy thing? A raisin? Raisins were definitely for old people — old people and kindergartners.

I was gagging on the raisin when Diego, Johnny, and José sat down.

"Don't let us interrupt your choking," Diego said.

"Yeah," said Johnny. "If you're choking, go ahead and choke. Don't let us stop you."

"Ha ha," I said. Not my most brilliant, but at least I was breathing.

"What are you doing at our table?" José said.

"I gotta tell Diego something."

They stared at me.

"In private."

Diego said, "Anything you can tell me, you can tell these guys. They're like brothers, ain't that right, José?"

"Hermanos," said José.

"Okay," I said, looking from Diego to Johnny to José.

"So?" said Diego.

"So there's these guys might ask you to go somewhere tonight. I don't know why, I think they're mad at somebody else and they want to use you as an example or something. So I don't think you should go."

106

I sounded like a five-year-old, babbling about good guys and bad guys. But Diego didn't laugh at me.

"You playin'? Who told you that?"

"Nobody," I said. "I overheard some stuff." That was true, right? Hiding behind a car eavesdropping was sort of like overhearing.

"Where you overhearing — in the jazz band?" He said it like a joke, but nobody laughed.

"No, I went with . . . my neighbor." Maybe I shouldn't tell him who was involved. Maybe I could help Diego without ratting out Daron.

"That little runty kid I see you with?"

Too late. "Yeah."

"You worried about him?" Johnny said. He and José laughed.

"No, his brother," I said. "He's in ninth grade. He's probably the one who would ask you to go somewhere, if anyone asked you. But probably no one will ask you. Just forget it."

This idea was getting more and more stupid. Just because Diego got me into jazz band and explained about my Phillies cap didn't mean I had to risk my life for him. And what would happen to Daron? Why had this ever seemed like a good idea?

"His brother that Daron kid I seen you with?"

"Yeah."

Diego glanced at Johnny and José. "Okay."

"Hey!" Johnny said. "I bet he means that kid came up to you in the hall!"

Diego looked at him harder. "I said okay."

"But he didn't ask you to go nowhere, he just said where you could meet up with . . . hey! Do you think it could be a setup?"

"You don't keep your mouth shut, I'll show you what's a setup."

"That better not be a threat to my friend Johnny," José said.

"I ain't threatening nobody," said Diego. "Just telling him information for his own good."

Just like I was trying to do. Why didn't I ever learn?

Johnny was in his own world.

"But maybe Ethan here's the setup. Maybe he tells you not to come, and when you don't come, pow!" Johnny punched the palm of his hand. "Bet you didn't think of that, did you?"

"Bet you didn't think who's going to have a fat lip in three seconds," Diego said.

Me? I wondered, but José was steering Johnny away from the table.

"Thanks for telling me," said Diego.

"So you're not going? To wherever you were gonna go?"

Diego paused. "I'll think about it. You gotta leave a guy alone when he's thinking."

"Okay. Sorry."

He stood up to join the crowd of kids stacking their trays on a metal shelf, and I stuffed my trash inside my plastic grocery bag.

How would I know when Diego was done thinking? He wouldn't tell me, but would there be a sign, like a code word, or a look on his face? I was on the lookout all day, but Diego wasn't giving hints.

⟨⟨⟨   ⟩⟩⟩

At my oboe lesson, I sounded like I had never held an instrument before. I put my fingers in the wrong places, breathed at the wrong times, and lost my place in the music. A couple of times, I squeaked so loud that I was sure other teachers would come in to see what animal was being slaughtered.

In the middle of "Boogie Woogie Santa Claus" Mr. Harper stopped me. "Mr. Oppenheimer, clearly your mind is not on your music today."

"No, it is," I insisted. Had Diego made a decision yet? "Last night I practiced for an hour."

"I didn't comment on your practice last night, Mr. Oppenheimer. I merely observed where your mind is not today."

109

"Oh."

"If we need to stop early, that might be advantageous for us both, unless, of course, there's some way I can help your mind return to its musical thoughts."

"Oh. No, I guess not."

"Hmm," said Mr. Harper. "You know, your oboe playing has progressed very well for such a short time."

"Thanks."

"How are you finding Parker as compared with your former school?"

"I don't know. It's different."

He wouldn't be interested in how kids dressed at Maple Heights Middle School, or the different words people used here. Felix calling my jacket "tight" meant something good, but back home people would think a "tight" jacket was just too small.

Finally I said, "The teachers are younger, but the books and stuff are older. It's weird."

"An astute observation."

"Thanks." I didn't know exactly what "astute" meant, but he was smiling, so I didn't think it was an insult.

"I'd be interested in more of your observations, any time you have any to share. I find that music is very much influenced by our observations of the world around us."

"Okay," I said, thinking about my observations from

the night before. I wasn't ready for them to influence my music.

When I got home I had another letter from Margo. This one was in a dark pink envelope, with the address written in silver pen. I still hadn't written her back from the first letter. Maybe after she mailed that one, she realized that it didn't say anything about home, so she had sent a P.S. I took it upstairs to my uncle's room, tipping the desk chair back as far as it would go as I read.

October 26

Ethan-beneathan,

Why am I not surprised you haven't written back yet? You better write soon! I'm just sending this because I thought you might be lonely down there with Grandma and Grandpa, especially without email. Although knowing you, you're probably friends with half of Washington by now. Have you gotten invited to dinner at the White House? (Ha ha)

I'm waiting for my laundry here in the basement of Addams Hall, which is really stupid but I know two people who've had jeans and stuff stolen out of the laundry room when they weren't down here watching. I guess when college costs this much, people have to save money somehow, but stealing clothes from people in your own dorm is pretty low.

Dad wanted to know what color to paint his walls (???) so he emailed me pictures of his apartment. I tried printing them out for you, but you couldn't really see anything on my dinky printer, and it was too weird a reason to go to a computer lab.

Dad's neighborhood in Old City is becoming totally artsy — not where I would have pictured him at all. Mom says it's the inner city, but what the hell is an inner city, anyway? Is your school in the inner city? How come no one ever talks about the outer city? Dad said the apartment has a microwave oven that you can leave voice messages on. (Not bad for the inner city.)

When are you going to talk to him again? You can't blame him forever, you know. You have a tendency to oversimplify things.

Clothes are clean. Gotta go. Write back!!!

Love,

Margo-from-Fargo

That letter, especially all those exclamation points, made me shove my math book off the desk. Oversimplifying? In math, wasn't the goal to simplify as much as possible? There was nothing simple about my dad decorating his own apartment. I thought about calling home, but my mom was probably at work, or having dinner with one of her friends at the Vietnamese restaurant near our house. She'd get home late and find my message on the machine, and if she called back, my grandparents would wake up and there would be shouting and chaos. Or she would decide it was too late to call back, which would be worse. Things that were so simple in other families, things like making phone calls, were so impossibly complicated in mine. You'd think a hotshot lawyer mom and a dad with a fancy "consulting" job (whatever that was) would have the brain power to figure out a simple thing like conversation, but apparently it was just too much for some people.

I don't know which I hated worse: being part of my family, or the fact that Margo thought we were normal.

12

Saturday morning, while my grandfather was at the retired pharmacists' breakfast, Mr. Taylor rang our doorbell. He wasn't the clean-shaven, ironed-shirt-and-necktie Mr. Taylor I saw leaving for work in the mornings, or the plaid-shirt-and-khaki Mr. Taylor who raked leaves on weekends. This Mr. Taylor looked like he hadn't slept in a year. His clothes were wrinkled, and his face was stubbly. Felix and Kameka were behind him, hanging back. Felix was biting the insides of his cheeks, and Kameka was staring at her pink sneakers.

"Mrs. Lowenstein, I'm sorry to intrude," Mr. Taylor said.

"It's no intrusion at all," my grandmother said. "Why don't you come in?"

"We can't stay. I just wonder if I might leave Kameka here for a couple of hours. It's — Daron's been hurt."

For just a second, my heart stopped beating.

"Oh dear," said my grandmother. "I hope he's all right."

I hoped so too. I really, really hoped so.

"So do we," said Mr. Taylor. "They're running some tests at the hospital, and we should know more tonight."

Felix tugged on his father's sleeve.

"Come on, Dad, visiting is only until three."

Mr. Taylor looked from Felix to my grandmother like he wanted to explain.

"Kameka and I can entertain ourselves as long as you need," said my grandmother, turning to her. "Would you like to help me bake an apple cake?"

Kameka nodded, but she looked more serious than excited. Felix looked serious too. He seemed to be looking everywhere except at me.

After Mr. Taylor and Felix left, my grandmother and Kameka started on the cake. I heard forks mixing against bowls, bowls clanking on counters, my grandmother humming. Through all the banging, I heard Kameka ask, "Why did bad people hurt my brother?"

That made my stomach felt sick, like the two poppy seed bagels and banana I ate that morning might rebel and fly across the room.

Around noon, my grandmother made Kameka and me grilled cheese sandwiches and tomato soup, like we were both four years old. Neither of us ate much. I reread a

Lone Ranger comic book until my grandfather came home. I heard my grandmother talking to him quietly.

At two-thirty, my grandfather was ready to go to the library. I brought a notebook, an info sheet about the project, and a pen. My grandfather brought a couple of magazines and the *Washington Post* "Style" section folded open to the crossword puzzle.

My grandfather didn't say anything about giving up his parking space. He also didn't complain about the bus in front of us that stopped at every corner. We listened to National Public Radio, where two guys were joking about car repairs. I kept thinking about Mr. Taylor's stubbly face and Daron lying in a hospital bed.

We could have parked around the corner from the library, but you had to feed the parking meters there, even on Saturday, and my grandfather said it was outrageous to pay for parking at a public library. So we parked four blocks away.

We got to the library at five after three. The lobby was cold and gray, like I imagined a prison lobby would look.

We stood for a minute near the metal detectors, and my grandfather said, "You sure your friend's going to come?"

"He's not my friend. But yeah, I'm sure."

"Well, I'll be on the first floor if he doesn't show and you want to go home early."

"He'll come."

"Good, then plan to meet me back here at five o'clock."

My grandfather emptied his pockets, went through the metal detector, and disappeared into the library. It was 3:08. How long should I wait for Diego? And if he didn't come, should I find my grandfather and leave or try to do the research myself? If Diego didn't come, my grandfather might not drive me back to the library again to meet him.

At 3:14, someone familiar walked in, but it wasn't who I was expecting. She didn't see me at first, but I was so relieved that I yelped out loud.

"Sharita?"

She turned around and smiled, a smile that was half-happy and half-confused. "What are you doing here?" she said.

"Waiting for Diego. We're supposed to do this project together, but I don't think he's coming."

"I'm here for that too. But Janeen and I are researching on our own. You know, so she doesn't have to be seen in public with me."

I must have looked puzzled because Sharita added, "You know, wouldn't want my *back*ground and all to damage her perfect image."

"But — "

"Forget it. Anyway, I'm going to the Washingtoniana

division for the March on Washington. You're doing the riots, right?"

How did she remember that?

"You should probably come to Washingtoniana too," she said.

3:19. Diego wasn't coming. Why had I ever tried to help him?

I followed Sharita through the metal detector, across a big room to an elevator. It was out of order so she led me past card catalogs, computers, and sale books to another bank of elevators. She pushed the button, and we heard an old-fashioned ding-ding as the elevator got closer.

The Washingtoniana Division was a room full of tables with people studying old maps and newspapers. We put our jackets at an empty table, and I followed Sharita to the librarian's desk.

"We're looking for information about the 1963 March on Washington and the 1968 riots," she said. "I mean, I'm doing the March, he's doing the riots."

The librarian smiled, like she had been hoping we'd stop by. She showed us each a couple of books, which we brought to our table, and then she gave us each a brown folder filled with newspaper clippings. I started rifling through mine.

"I've seen some of these pictures before," I told her. "Like this one of the police and the teargas."

"Where?"

"At my grandparents' house. My mom made this scrapbook about events in 1968, and it has some of these pictures in it."

"Why?" she asked.

"Who knows? My mom's in Pennsylvania, and the scrapbook was in my uncle's room but he's dead."

"Sorry."

"No, I didn't know him. He died of a bad reaction to some medicine when he was twenty."

"Some medicine or *some* medicine?" Sharita smiled.

"What do you mean?"

"I mean, twenty-year-old guys sometimes self-prescribe their own medicine."

I hadn't thought of that before.

"Don't worry about it," said Sharita.

For the next hour, we focused on our projects. I learned more than I ever wanted to know about the city going crazy after Martin Luther King, Jr., was killed in 1968. I looked at photos of businesses on fire, on Seventh and Fourteenth Streets. I wished I could remember where my grandfather said he'd worked.

After an hour, I took a chance. I turned to Sharita.

"I had fun studying with you," I said.

Sharita smiled. "Yeah, riots are the best."

"No, I mean — "

"I know. I had fun too."

We both reached for a book at the same time, and our hands accidentally brushed each other's. *Bzzzt!* Then, like nothing had happened, we carried the books to the reshelving cart at the end of an aisle.

"Let's take the stairs down," said Sharita.

She pulled open the door to the stairwell, but I didn't know it was a pull door instead of a push and I didn't step back quickly enough. For a second, our whole bodies were touching, and a jolt of energy raced through all of my blood vessels. I imagined holding her in my arms in a slow dance.

The stairwell was a gray, empty space that looked even older than the rest of the library. A fluorescent light buzzed, making the stairwell look like something from a science fiction movie. But with Sharita there, it was the most romantic place in the world.

We lingered at the top of the stairs. We looked at each other. Then, without even knowing who started it or when, why, or how, our lips were touching. Hers were warm and soft and had the energy of a thousand buzzing light bulbs.

After the kiss, I followed Sharita's lead and sat down on the top step. I would have sat anywhere she wanted, even somewhere where we could get stepped on or trampled. I was the happiest person alive —

"Ethan, why are you here?" she asked me.

— for about a second.

"We've got this — " my voice tripped on itself, and I cleared my throat. "We have a social studies project. I'm doing the riots. You know, Diego didn't — "

"You know what I mean. Why'd you come to D.C.?"

Sharita was wearing one black and silver sock and one red and green striped sock. The way she was sitting, with her knees bent and her notebook on her lap, she looked like a sculpture. She was staring straight ahead, like there was something to see on the wall of the stairwell. "Girl in Library," the sculpture would be called.

Then I told her. Of all the stupid, idiotic things I could have done in that stairwell, I told her why I was in D.C.

"See, okay. Okay, there was this kid, right? At my old school? His name was Alex. His family moved here from Russia in third grade, and they didn't know a lot about America. Like how boys don't wear Hello Kitty shirts. Or, if you eat a hot dog for lunch, you don't eat it cold out of your lunchbox, and you don't eat it on white bread."

"He ate hot dogs on white bread?"

"Yeah! I don't know if they did that in Russia, or if they thought that's what Americans did, but it was funny. Kids used to call him 'hot dog boy,' but he didn't know enough English to know they were being mean."

"That's sad."

"I guess, but he didn't know. He ran around the play-ground yelling 'hot dog boy' like everybody else."

Sharita stretched her legs in front of her. These stairs weren't as comfortable as the ones at school — they were harder and colder. I shifted my weight.

"So how did some kid in third grade make you come to D.C. five years later?"

"Right. So, he got more normal the longer his family lived here. Last year they even moved out of their apart-ment into a house on my street, and he has a little brother who was born here. Totally normal."

"Why is your street more normal than their apart-ment?"

"Well, it's not — it's just, you know, they were settling in."

"Uh huh."

I moved away from the apartment-versus-house topic.

"Anyway, he was okay. His dad gave me a ride to school sometimes. But kids still thought he was different, you know, even though he wasn't anymore. So if he had asked anyone, I mean, anyone would've told him it was a bad idea to ask out this girl, Mary Anne Kaplowski."

"Why?"

"Well, she's just — she's one of those girls. You know. The kind of person who decides what everybody else should do."

I don't know why some girls follow each other around like sheepdogs, but that's how they were with Mary Anne. I didn't mind in seventh grade when she decided they should let their bra straps show a little, but this was different.

"So he asked her out and she said no?"

"Well, she didn't just say no. She called him a sexual predator and started this thing where everyone had to avoid him."

I remembered her in the cafeteria shrieking, "Molester!" with everyone at her table giggling hysterically.

"How do you know he wasn't? All those Hello Kitty shirts or whatever."

"No, he — he just wasn't. Definitely not. It was just this thing where Mary Anne had to be the center of everything, and he set himself up by asking her out."

"Okay."

"So everyone kind of attacked him."

"Attacked him?"

"It was stupid at first, poking him to see if they could make him flinch, stupid stuff. Writing him notes that said 'Molester!' But then the girls wanted to get their boyfriends involved. To protect them or whatever."

"What did they do to him?" Sharita said. I liked the way she said "they," like I definitely was not involved.

"Well, that's when it got worse. A couple of times my friend Josh hid behind a bush and tried to hit him with pebbles while he waited outside for his ride to pick him up, but it was like — "

"He tried to hit the boy with rocks?"

I remembered the shady area outside the school, where people stood around waiting for their moms to pick them up from after-school clubs. There was a parade of minivans and SUVs every day, with bumper stickers bragging about their kids. Everyone just prayed their mom would stay in the car.

"Pebbles. But it was like — "

"And you were friends with this guy?"

"Never mind," I said.

"No, go on. Your friend used to pitch rocks."

"Pebbles!" Why had I told her any of this?

"Pebbles."

"Plus, I was friends with this kid since we were three. We didn't become friends because I was into the pebbles."

"No, you just thought it didn't matter as long as he didn't actually hit the kid."

"No!" How did she know I had thought that? "But, actually, he did hit him, a few of them got the back of his legs."

I glanced at Sharita, and she was staring at me like I had run over her pet kitten. Any idiot would have quit talking then, found some reason to change the subject, or left the building, but not me. I still thought I could make her understand.

She asked, "So why did Alex just stand there?"

"That's what we wondered!" She did understand me! "But now that I'm here, I kind of can see — I mean, you don't want the other guys to think you're weak. Like you can't take it."

"Uh-huh."

"So it was hard to know when things kind of crossed the line."

"Throwing rocks didn't cross the line?"

"Pebbles!"

"Whatever. Where were you these times your friend was hiding behind the bush?"

"Well, there were a lot of bushes. Flowers and stuff. There was room for a lot of people."

Besides me and Josh, Caleb and Tyler were there. If we looked through the bushes to the left, we saw the school building, one story and sprawling, windows alternating with bright blue panels. To our right, the teachers' cars reflected the late afternoon sun. And straight ahead, kids waited to be picked up. Lots of kids at first, then fewer, and then just Alex Krashevsky. My legs cramped up, and it got boring, sitting there trying not to get scratched by the branches.

"I can't believe you had flowers at your school and you stood around throwing rocks at people. It's barbaric."

"Forget it, then. End of story. That's why I came to D.C."

"That's not the end of the story!"

"How would you know? You're not even listening." I wanted to go back to kissing, or even back to working on our social studies projects.

But Sharita said, "You're right. I'm sorry," and her eyes were so big and deep I couldn't help telling her the rest.

"Okay, so this one afternoon, they were like, 'Here, throw these.' And I didn't want to, but I could kind of see their point, like why was I back there if I wasn't part of it, like I was either their friend or not, you know? So I decided I would do it, but I'd be careful not to hit him."

I remembered thinking that. I remembered being the person who thought that, but I wasn't that person anymore. It was like visiting an elementary school and not believing you were ever small enough to drink from those water fountains.

"So let me guess," Sharita said.

"Yeah. No. See, that was when he finally reacted. He turned around to come over to us, and that's when he slipped on all these pebbles."

Sharita stared at me.

"He never even got hit. He tripped and fell down, but he didn't get hit."

"So he was fine?"

I paused. "Well — his legs got torn up from landing on the pebbles, and — "

"His legs got torn up through his pants?"

"He was wearing shorts. It was the beginning of this year, the second week of school. In September."

"Shorts to school? Man, you kids in Maple Wherever just do whatever the hell you want, don't you?"

"First of all, it's Maple Heights, and second of all, we don't do whatever we want."

"And?"

I looked at her.

"You started to say 'and,' like it wasn't just his legs got torn up."

I didn't want to tell her any more, but it was too late. I didn't know how to stop what I had started.

"I — he — when he fell, he also hit his head on a — there was a metal bike rack in the area where we were waiting."

Before that day, I had never noticed that bike rack. And I had never, ever seen anyone ride a bike to Maple Heights Middle School.

Sharita stared at me.

"He's okay now," I told her. "I mean, he was lucky. We

were all lucky. He was in the hospital for, like, three or four days, but his head and everything, he's okay now."

"Lucky for him you live such a charmed life."

"I guess."

I didn't know how to take that, but I was too tired to disagree. It was like I was there again, only this time I could zoom in on the details. I saw the cheap sneakers Alex was wearing, navy blue with a white design, and how his hair was too long in the back, and the wind blew through it as he waited for his ride.

I remembered other details too: my legs hurting from squatting behind that bush; the coolness of dirt when I reached down to pick up that first pebble; the voices of kids on the spirit team drifting around the side of the school.

That day, I was supposed to be at the orthodontist getting fitted for braces, but my mom had changed my appointment and forgotten to tell me. It was a Tuesday, so the cleaning lady would still be at home, so I wouldn't have wanted to go there and be in her way even if I knew the appointment had changed. Nothing wrong with just hanging out, I told myself. And when Tyler said I was either in or out, I decided nothing bad would happen if I threw some pebbles, just into the air, not at anything in particular. I remembered releasing those first couple of pebbles like animals into the wild, setting them free.

Alex had nothing to do with it. It was about me and the dirt and the pebbles, sitting behind a bush on a cool September afternoon in my last year of middle school. I didn't care how he ate his hot dogs or if he went out with Mary Anne Kaplowski. I thought I didn't care if his mother waved hello to me outside her house.

I took a breath and went on.

"So my friends, my so-called friends who were with me, Josh and Tyler and Caleb, they took off. They ran so fast it was like they were never there."

"So why didn't you run?"

For the first time I was glad I hadn't.

"Well, part of me thought that would be smart. But part of me was like, there's a guy on the ground who's hurt. Someone should help him, or at least wait and see if he's okay."

I heard the elevator creak in the wall behind us.

"So what did you do?" Sharita said.

"Well, I was standing there, making up my mind, when the police and the ambulance came at the same time."

"Someone called the police over that? The police in Maple Heights must not have a lot to do."

"I guess. But then Alex starts shouting from the ground, 'That's him, that's the kid who threw rocks at me.'"

I waited for Sharita to say, "I thought it was pebbles," but she didn't.

"At first I thought it was good that Alex was yelling, because it meant he was conscious and everything, but then I realized what he was saying, and that it was true. At first they were gonna press charges and then it was going to be a lawsuit, but then the lawyers settled or whatever, so it's nothing."

"And the other guys never got caught?"

"I thought telling would make things worse."

"So you came here?"

Sharita's arms were folded across her chest. She was no longer "Girl in Library" but "Supreme Court Justice on the Stairs."

"Yeah. Well, are you sure you want to hear this?"

"Oh, I'm sure."

"Well, I got suspended, and everyone acted like they hadn't all been doing the same thing. They treated me like a criminal or something."

"Like you know what that's like."

I paused. Was I supposed to ask her more? I didn't know what to ask, so I kept talking.

"Nobody answered my calls or IMs, and finally my friend Josh sent me a one-sentence email to say nobody's parents were letting them talk to me. Like I was a bad influence or something. And I've known Josh since I was three! Plus I wasn't even — I mean, I was just doing what the rest of them were doing. It wasn't even my idea."

Sharita said more in her silence than most people said in an hour of talking. I couldn't stand it and rushed to fill the empty air.

"So that's why I'm here — I guess it was hard on my mom, having everyone think she was a terrible parent or whatever, for having a kid like me. And I guess my grandparents were the only ones who would take me."

"No dad, huh? I assumed you had a dad."

"I do have a dad."

"Uh huh," said Sharita. A pause. "So, sucks for you, living down here."

I didn't want to insult her. "Well, it's not as bad as I thought it would be. I guess I'm kind of getting used to it."

"Oh," Sharita said. "Well, maybe you shouldn't get too used to things."

"Things, meaning . . . ?"

"Meaning, part of me likes you, but you're not like I thought you were. I know enough people who do stupid things and have to plan their life around court dates."

It felt like the stairwell had collapsed and buried me in an avalanche of old books nobody wanted to read.

"But — "

"I gotta go," Sharita said. "They don't like me being out after dark."

I couldn't think of anything to say.

"Bye, Ethan."

"Bye."

I still had ten minutes until I had to meet my grandfather. I didn't want to be early in case he asked why, so I went back to the Washingtoniana Division and walked up and down the aisles until it was time to take the elevator downstairs.

When we got home, my grandmother said there was a message that my dad had called. But there was no way I was calling him back.

13

Daron was in the hospital two days with a broken arm, a dislocated shoulder, and complications from his asthma that got worse from the other stuff. Felix and I walked to school together in the mornings, and Mr. Taylor picked Felix up in the afternoons so they could visit Daron. My grandmother made them a chicken casserole.

"Stupid neighborhood," Felix said on the way to school.

I hesitated before asking, but I had to know if this had to do with Diego. "Who did it? Do you know?"

Felix shrugged.

"Guys. Friends of the guys we saw that night."

"Why?"

"'Cause they're stupid. 'Cause they don't know his brother knows karate and is gonna karate-chop their heads off." Felix did a couple of practice moves in the air.

"But did he — do you know why they did it?"

Felix looked at me sideways.

"I can't ask him nothing 'cause my dad's always there. But when he gets home from the hospital, I'm gonna find out who did this to him and — " he didn't finish. He just let out a long sigh.

When Daron did come home, he couldn't even eat.

"Why isn't he eating?" I asked.

"I don't know," Felix said. "We had your grandmother's chicken what's-it-called last night, and that was good! Kameka had seconds, and usually she only likes chicken if it's nuggets."

It was the first positive thing anybody had said about my grandmother's food. But Felix didn't say anything else the rest of the way to school. Whenever I looked at him, he was making strange faces, with his eyes squinched up and his jaw stretching to the side. He was still trying to wiggle his ears.

Sharita was absent from school a couple of days, and when she was there she ignored me. I hated how she always had to be right, and how she got angry so easily. I hated how she let me explain about Maple Heights, practically pour out my life story to her, and then used it against me. After pretending she was my friend, even kissing me! I made sure not to look sideways in science, so I didn't see her out of the corner of my eye. In jazz band, I focused harder on my sheet music so I couldn't see her leg stretched out and her foot tapping to the beat.

‹‹‹   ›››

While Daron was recovering and Sharita was ignoring me, I got two more notes from Margo. I had meant to write her back from before, but the longer I waited, the more complicated everything got, and the more impossible to explain in a letter. At first I thought I wanted her to tell me about home, even though she wasn't even living there. But the more she said about our parents and whatever was or wasn't going on in their marriage, the harder it got to write back. Her note was on the back of an orange flyer about an alcohol awareness program.

November 13

Ethan-good-griefen,

Okay, it's kind of not funny anymore that you haven't written back! Did you even get my other letters? You better not be lazy and not write back because it's too hard to ask Grandma and Grandpa for an envelope and a stamp. It's not my fault you can't get to your email. (Can't you check it on a computer in the library or something? I've sent you, like, twenty jokes, mostly from Uncle Frank.) Anyway, write me back or don't, whatever. But this is the last letter you're getting from me until you do.

Anyway, the reason I'm writing is *just in case* the reason you didn't write back is that I hurt your feelings over asking whether your school is in the "inner city." I didn't mean it in a bad way. I think the school where I tutor is sort of "inner city." Does your school at least have soap and paper towels in the bathrooms???

Everyone's getting a sweatshirt for Hanukkah this year, so if you don't want yours to be an XS in pink, you better write back and tell me what size you are now.

Love,

Milagro Margo

The next day, another letter came.

"Poor girl must be lonely so far away," my grandmother said as she handed me the envelope. "I always forget, is it three hours earlier or three hours later in California?"

"If Margo waited to mail her letter until she finished what she had to say, she could put everything in one envelope and save a stamp," my grandfather said. "College students didn't used to run around like they had all this money."

I took the letter upstairs to my uncle's desk and decided to read it later. I could find my way around the room in the dark now, and I didn't stub my toe on the dresser anymore. It helped, I guess, that I didn't have piles of stuff everywhere like in my room at home. After dinner we watched the news, and then I practiced the oboe.

But I didn't practice long. Every note reminded me of jazz band, and jazz band reminded me of Sharita. And then I got to thinking that Sharita was right about me being a jerk. I had caused problems for Alex Krashevsky, and now I had caused even worse problems for Daron by telling Diego not to show up. The oboe squeaked and squawked for another few minutes before I gave up. I was hopeless. I packed up my instrument as fast as I could and brushed my teeth to get rid of the taste. That's when I remembered Margo's note.

November 14

E —

This is just a P.S. to yesterday's letter, because I meant what I said about not writing until you write back. But I wanted to tell you something my roommate JoJo learned in her sociology class. She said a lot of couples wait until the first child starts college before they get divorced. I asked her how many couples who "try" separation end up getting divorced, but she didn't know. Mom and Dad wouldn't do that, would they? It's hard to find times to call when it's not after midnight on the East Coast, and whenever I call (house or apartment), neither one of them is ever home. So I don't know what's going on.

Love,

M

That letter I didn't save. I crumpled it into a ball and buried it in my trash can under some dirty tissues.

14

Lately whenever I practiced the oboe I ended up thinking about things I didn't want to, like my family and the people I knew here. After a while I couldn't stand it. I couldn't skip jazz band, but I didn't have to give it extra time either. So I stopped going to oboe lessons for about a week.

One day at the end of band, Mr. Harper came up to me while I was taking apart my oboe.

"Mr. Oppenheimer?"

"Yeah?" Mr. Harper kept looking at me. "I mean, yes."

What was it with adults who didn't care how kids treated each other but got all worked up if someone said "yeah?" instead of "yes"?

"Do you have a moment?"

I ran a swab through the oboe to clean out the spit.

"I have to go to science."

"And I have a dog named Spiffy, but that doesn't answer my question."

What kind of name was Spiffy for a dog?

"Okay." I put the reed, the swab, and the oboe pieces in the case and closed it with a snap.

"Mr. Oppenheimer, I haven't seen you after school all week," he said.

I picked up the oboe case, but the end of the swab had gotten caught in the lid. I had to undo the clasps and open it again.

"I've been busy," I said. No way could I tell him what was really going on, not that it was his business.

He put up his hand.

"Mr. Oppenheimer, I'm not suggesting you regale me with your after-school adventures. I am merely informing you of a polite courtesy you might impart if someone is expecting you for an appointment."

"Oh. Sorry. I just — I guess I got busy and forgot."

"When we are busiest," said Mr. Harper, "is sometimes when it is most important to make time for music."

"It's just so . . . pointless," I said, without thinking.

"Pointless how?"

"Well, it's just — there's so many real problems. No offense, I mean, music is cool, but it's not going to solve anything in the world."

I had never talked this way to a teacher before. I couldn't tell if he looked mad or interested.

"Mr. Oppenheimer," he said, "I am the oldest of seven

children. My parents were Irish farmers who came here and worked all their lives. University isn't free here like it is in Ireland. My trumpet-playing not only brought me to university but also helped me pay for a brother and a sister to study as well." He paused, ruffling through a stack of sheet music. "Solving the *world's* problems I don't know about, but music did an excellent job of solving my problems."

I didn't know how to answer that.

"I admire you thinking big, Mr. Oppenheimer, but sometimes we get so caught up in what we can't do that we forfeit what we might do. And what you might do, with a great deal of practice, is play a damn good oboe."

I had never heard a teacher say "damn" before.

"Thanks," I said.

"Don't thank me unless I should expect to see you after school."

"Okay." I sighed as he wrote me a pass to science.

Who said I wanted to be a great oboe player anyway? Music might have helped Mr. Harper with his problems, but it hadn't helped me in Maple Heights and it wasn't helping in Washington. On the other hand, oboe lessons were practically the only thing my grandparents let me out of the house for.

Walking down the hall, I kicked every third locker. I stopped when I saw Sharita on the floor, surrounded by piles of scattered paper. One of her socks had dangling silver bells.

I started to walk past her, thinking it was stupid to help someone who was mad at me, but then I stopped. I couldn't help it.

"What's going on?" I asked her.

"Notebook popped. What are you doing here?"

"Talking to Mr. Harper."

I handed her a stack of her science notes.

"Thanks. I've been trying to convince Ms. Franklin to let me make up math quizzes. I've been absent for, like, the last five, but she's only letting me make up three," she said.

"That's a lot of quizzes."

I handed her some book reports.

"What were you and Mr. Harper talking about?"

"Music. Whether it solves anything or not."

"Sounds deep." She took a handful of papers and tapped them on the floor to even out the edges.

"Yeah. It's just stupid, 'cause, like, you need school to get a job or whatever, but why do you need music? With kids getting killed on the street and stuff, maybe I should be doing something more useful after school."

I hadn't meant to talk to her like this, but I was still worked up from my conversation with Mr. Harper, and I had forgotten how easy she was to talk to.

"Like what, PlayStation?"

Sharita knew how to get me mad. She didn't even know about my PlayStation back in Maple Heights, how that day after Alex Krashevsky, I had thrown my backpack down in frustration and the PlayStation had broken. It looked okay on the outside, but when you turned it on, it made a sad humming sound and wouldn't play games.

"You think you're so perfect, but you're not," I said, anger boiling up inside. It felt like somebody else was talking using my mouth and vocal cords. Sharita stared up at me, and something made me keep going.

"I mean, you act like because I made one mistake, you can't talk to me anymore. Like I'll bring you down or something. And it's the same with everyone else — I mean, maybe some of them do look down on your family, like you say, but you spend a lot of time looking down on them too, you know, rejecting them before they can reject you."

I hadn't known I thought those things, but as I said them I knew they were true. Sharita stood up, her arms folded across her chest, not saying anything. I had screwed up ever getting to talk to her again (forget about kissing her), but I didn't care. For the first time in my life, I didn't care what somebody else thought of me.

When I turned to walk away, Sharita's sock jingled behind me.

"Ethan, wait," she called. "I'm not saying you're right

143

or wrong about the other kids. But you — I mean, yeah, you did make one mistake. One huge mistake. But this is the first time, until today . . . I mean, you never said anything about wanting to fix things. I mean, maybe not fix things but at least do something good in the world to balance it out."

I shrugged.

"What did you mean before, about doing something useful?"

"I don't know," I said. "Nothing."

"Nothing, like, you don't want to, or nothing, like, you don't think you can?"

I knew this was a test, and if I answered right she might be friends with me again. I told the truth. "The second one, I guess."

"Why, 'cause we're young?" Sharita said.

"Yeah."

"Well, I don't feel like a kid. And the adults I know aren't doing much better. What did any of them do to help your neighbor?"

She knew about Daron?

"I know, but — " I said.

"So do something, you know? If you don't want to be one of those grown-ups who sits around and complains, then do something. I'm sick of people telling me how hard their life is, then not doing anything about it."

Sharita had gotten her notebook assembled, and we walked slowly to class.

"You know how I started playing the trombone?" she said. "We had my dad's trombone at our house, but no one knew how to play it. Then some high school kids came to my third grade class with their instruments and stuff, like to get us interested. They gave us this paper where if your parents signed it, you could go on Saturdays for free music lessons at Duke Ellington School. So I got this lady at the library to sign for me, and I went there for three years, until I was too old."

"That's cool."

"I always said I was gonna do something like that, when I got to high school. Something to get little kids like me into music instead of other stuff."

"Yeah, that would be good," I said.

When Mr. Harper talked about music changing things it was hard to imagine, but it sounded better, easier when Sharita said it.

"But why should we wait 'til high school?" Sharita said.

"Yeah," I said. "I bet Mr. Harper would let us go to an elementary school and show them our instruments."

"Let's ask him this afternoon. You staying after for an oboe lesson?"

"Yes!" I said, much more enthusiastically than I had said it to Mr. Harper. "I mean, yeah. I'm staying."

When we said goodbye, she smiled at me a second or two longer than necessary.

《《《　》》》

When I got to the band room after school, Sharita was waiting for me, doing science homework at a desk.

"He didn't believe me that you were coming," she said.

Mr. Harper had his back to us. He was pulling folders out of a file cabinet.

"I don't recall expressing a belief one way or the other," he said, glancing over his shoulder at me. "However, it is certainly a pleasure to see you, Mr. Oppenheimer."

"I told him we had an idea," Sharita said, "but I didn't tell him what it was."

"Okay," I said, and then there was a pause.

"Well, I guess we were thinking — " I said at the same time Sharita said, "Ethan and I think — " and then we both stopped. This was too important to mess up.

Mr. Harper turned around, leaned his back against the file cabinet, and looked at us. The corners of his mouth looked like they were fighting back a smile.

"Go ahead," I said.

"No, you tell him."

"Okay, well, Sharita was in this program — "

"It was this thing when I was in elementary school," she interrupted.

Eventually we got it out. We told him about Sharita's trombone and the free music lessons, although she left out the part about the librarian signing her permission slip. Mr. Harper nodded his head and said, "Mm-hmm, mm-hmm," like he was talking to grownups.

When we had finished, Mr. Harper looked pleased.

"You know, there's a group that does some work collecting used instruments and things for children," he said. "The tuba player in the band I play with volunteers with them. Why don't I make a few phone calls and see what I can learn?"

"Okay," I said, while Sharita said, "That would be great."

"Admirable of you to suggest it," said Mr. Harper with a sharp nod of his head. "Now, shall we see about that oboe?"

‹‹‹   ›››

The next morning, Mr. Harper called Sharita and me out of homeroom. He stood next to his desk with his hands behind his back, smiling like someone had offered the Parker jazz band a recording deal.

"Great news!" he said.

"Did you call the tuba player?" Sharita asked. She remembered details like that, like what instrument Mr.

147

Harper's friend played. She probably knew what socks she had worn to school every day for the past month.

"Indeed I did," Mr. Harper beamed.

He handed us some stapled-together pages printed from a website. The first page in the packet said "Hungry for Music" and had a picture of a CD with a bite out of it.

"What do they do?" Sharita asked.

Mr. Harper read from their mission statement: "They inspire disadvantaged children and others by bringing positive musical and creative experiences into their lives."

"The tuba player tells me they are amenable to donations, that oftentimes groups hold concerts to benefit the organization."

I wasn't exactly sure what "amenable" meant, but I got the idea.

"We could have a concert and raise money for elementary kids to do music?" I asked.

"People would *pay* to hear us play?" Sharita said.

Mr. Harper shrugged. "That would be for you to decide."

"Would we get to organize it?" Sharita asked.

"With appropriate staff supervision," said Mr. Harper.

"Does that mean no dirty songs?" I said, trying to be funny. They both gave me a look.

"Let's talk more about it today in class," Mr. Harper said as he wrote us a pass to first period.

In the hall, Sharita and I were quiet at first. I wanted to tell her I liked her socks (one blue and white striped, one with Coca-Cola logos), or that I was glad we were doing the Hungry for Music project, or that I was sorry for my stupid joke about dirty songs. Even if I knew any, I wouldn't play dirty songs on the oboe.

Sharita finally said, "I'm glad we're doing this Hungry for Music thing."

"Me too. I like your socks." There.

She laughed. Sharita was beautiful when she laughed, her white teeth against her dark lips, and her eyes behind the purple glasses looking like each one held a million jazz expressions.

"You're crazy," she said, still laughing. "Totally crazy."

‹‹‹   ›››

Mr. Harper began jazz band with an announcement. "I believe two of your classmates have an idea they would like to run past you."

He looked at me, and at Sharita over my head. The radiator hissed, and in the back corner, one of the lights flickered. Neither of us said anything at first, and then we both started talking at once.

"Mr. Harper knows about this organization — "

"We were thinking it would be cool to, like, do something with our music — "

We had barely finished explaining when people started talking like it was a sure thing.

"How much money are we gonna raise?"

"Can we give some instruments to my sister's school?"

"After this, can we go on tour and raise money for instruments in other places?"

It took twenty minutes to hear everyone's suggestions. Mr. Harper decided we could spend part of class every Friday organizing our concert, but in the meantime we had to work on sounding good.

Like Mr. Harper said, we had to put some soul into our music.

15

Thanksgiving was boring. Boring and stupid and point-less. Thanksgiving was always a little boring and stupid, but at least when my mom put marshmallows in the sweet potatoes, it wasn't totally pointless.

For dinner, my grandmother used fancy plates with flowers around the edges. We had individual turkey breasts (dry) with string beans (mushy) and a baked sweet potato (not all that sweet). We did have a pecan pie with whipped cream, which was okay. Afterward, I was scrap-ing bits of food off our plates into a plastic bag my grand-mother keeps near the sink instead of a garbage disposal, when the phone rang. It was on the wall above my grand-father's head.

"I think we've gotten more phone calls in the past two months than we got all of last year," he grumbled, not making any attempt to answer it.

"Ira, can you get that, please?" my grandmother said.

She was wiping moisture off the apple juice bottle with a slightly used paper towel.

"Hello?" he said into the receiver. Pause. "Hello? You'll have to talk a little louder." Another pause. Then a smile took over his face. "Margo? Margo, sweetie, how ya doing?"

It didn't matter that he probably couldn't hear most of what Margo was saying. He looked like he had won the lottery, an Academy Award, and a Nobel Prize. I sighed. That's what she got for being the kind of person who kept in touch, for sending little cards and letters to my grandparents all these years. Nobody's face ever looked like that from hearing my voice.

"Wonderful talking to you, sweetie. Hold on, I'm going to put your grandmother on." He handed the phone to my grandmother, adding, "It's Margo!"

"It's so good to hear your voice, sweetheart," my grandmother was saying. "Now, what time is it there? I can't keep it straight. Uh huh. Well, she sounds like a very nice girl. Taiwan, you say? Do they have Thanksgiving in Taiwan?"

If the Pilgrims and Indians had met up in Taiwan, we'd eat moo shu turkey every year, which wouldn't be so bad. I hadn't had Chinese food in a long time.

"Uh huh, well, of course you want to talk to your brother. I think it's so nice you've been sending him those notes. I don't know what it is with boys and writing letters. Do you know that when your grandfather was in the war, I got three letters in six months? I wrote him five letters a week, and I got three letters the whole time. You know what, though, honey?" Pause. "It doesn't mean they don't love you if they don't write back."

My grandmother looked at me and shook her head.

"You know, Ethan reminds me more and more of your grandfather every day." Another pause. "You? I thought you knew that, honey, you're your mother's daughter all the way. I swear sometimes — but this is costing you money!"

Pause.

"I don't care if it's a calling card, unless calling cards are growing on trees out there." Pause. "All right, do you have enough minutes to talk to your brother?"

My grandmother gestured wildly for me to come to the phone, like gold was draining through the wires every second the line was silent.

"Hi, Margo."

"Ethan!" Her voice was like a hug. "Happy Thanksgiving. How come you didn't write back?"

"I don't know. Happy Thanksgiving." My toes stretched back and forth inside my socks. In the background, I heard running water and my grandmother scrubbing dishes.

"It's weird not being home," she said. "I mean, it totally made sense not to go home for such a short time, but it's still weird not being there."

"Did Grandma say you're going to Taiwan?" Taiwan wasn't that much farther than California, was it?

"No, doofus, I'm at my roommate's house in Santa Cruz. Her family is from Taiwan."

"Oh."

There was a half-second pause then. Someone who didn't know Margo wouldn't have even noticed. But Margo never paused. She could go outside to get the mail and talk to Mrs. Krashevsky for twenty minutes about three-bean salad. That was almost seven minutes per bean.

"I talked to Mom this morning," she said.

"Yeah? How is she?" My grandfather was sitting next to me, turning the pages of the newspaper loudly. My grandmother was packaging leftovers into old margarine containers.

"She's . . . okay," Margo said.

Another pause.

"I think they're going to, you know, go ahead with the divorce."

"What?"

My grandmother glanced at me from the counter near the sink, and I lowered my voice.

"But they haven't — I mean, it hasn't been that long since the — " I couldn't even say the word "separation."

"Well, Mom said they were just, what was it? 'Postponing the inevitable.'"

That sounded like the name of a bad soap opera. I stepped aside so my grandfather could leave the kitchen.

"So, when . . . ?" I said.

"I don't know. They have to file some papers and stuff with their lawyers. It could take a while."

"But — " I felt like I was four years old again, climbing into bed with Margo because I thought I heard thunder. It had actually been our neighbor's drunk teenage son riding their power mower around on their lawn. Now I was almost as old as that guy had been, but I was still hoping Margo could fix things.

"Yeah," she said. "So maybe it's good you're in Washington."

"Maybe."

I picked up a fork from the table and twirled it around in my fingers. I heard my grandfather flush the toilet in the hall bathroom. Of course my grandparents already knew, I realized. They probably knew back when they agreed to let me live here. Why was I always the last one to know everything? I couldn't believe they hadn't told me, though I don't know what they would have said: "Hey, newsflash, your parents are getting divorced. It's probably all that spicy ethnic food."

"Um, I should probably go," Margo said. "Sorry to ruin your Thanksgiving."

"It's okay." A pause. "Hey, Margo?"

"Yeah?"

"Those letters where you sounded all happy and stuff, making jokes — "

"Jokes?"

"Yeah, I mean, you agree that this sucks, right?"

"This totally sucks."

"Okay."

Hearing her say that made me feel about ten times better. Or maybe two times better. But after we hung up I wondered, could Margo be wrong? Maybe my mom had called on her cell phone and said she was getting a horse, but there was static and Margo had misheard. The only way to know for sure was to call my mom. If she was even home. I ran up the stairs two at a time without explaining to my grandmother.

"Hello?" My mother's voice sounded far away.

"Mom?"

"Ethan! I was going to call you, I just — what time is it?"

"Five-fifteen. Uh, I talked to Margo . . ."

"Did you? Good. She was so worried she hadn't heard

from you. I told her not to worry, but you know how she is."

"Yeah. Well, she mentioned — she said she had talked to you."

A pause. "Mm-hmm."

Was she going to make me say it?

"Ethan, honey."

"Yeah?"

"Sweetie, I didn't mean for you to find out like this."

"Find out what?"

My mom sighed.

"Sweetie, this . . . 'trial separation' wasn't working for either your father or me."

"So what are you going to do? There's lots of things you could do," I said.

She hadn't used the word "divorce," and I wasn't going to let her hang up the phone without saying it. Why should I make things easier on her than I had to? I twisted the phone cord around my finger, and it left a red mark when I released it.

"Ethan, sweetie, your dad and I are getting divorced. I didn't mean for you to find out this way."

"Then why are you doing it, if you didn't want me to find out?"

"I know you have a lot going on right now, and you don't need this as one more thing — "

"You don't know what I need! You have no idea," I said.

"Ethan, sweetie — "

"I gotta go. That's what I need."

I banged the receiver down on the phone, which I had never done before. My parents had never gotten divorced before, either. And they wouldn't have even bothered mentioning it to me if I hadn't called. My mom was the worst communicator ever. I thought about that day I was standing outside Maple Heights Middle School, waiting for my mom to take me to an orthodontist appointment she forgot to tell me had changed. And how she "forgot" she hadn't mentioned the possibility of me going to school in D.C. No wonder my dad wanted a microwave oven that talked — probably his new microwave was a better communicator than my mom was. Maybe everything wasn't my dad's fault. Maybe Margo was right about how I sometimes oversimplified things.

For the rest of Thanksgiving weekend, I mostly played the oboe. I had thought the oboe was the one thing that couldn't make me feel worse, but I was wrong. Every time my mind wandered back to my parents, the oboe squawked like a parrot, or like the mechanical donkey on my old See-and-Say toy: "the donkey says dee-vorce." It wasn't music at all.

There were other sounds in my grandparents' house aside from the oboe, not that they sounded much better.

There were announcers on National Public Radio, a vacuum cleaner, my grandfather yelling how he couldn't hear his program. Bathroom noises, scissors clipping coupons, water filling up an old plastic watering can. My grandmother yelling for my grandfather to move his coupons, and my grandfather yelling that if she didn't over-water the plants, he could cut coupons anywhere he wanted without them getting wet. I listened to it all — anything to drown out thoughts about my parents. And Sharita. And Diego and Daron and Felix. And the oboe — what made me think I could play the oboe in front of hundreds of people in a concert, let alone raise money for Hungry for Music? Even thoughts about my uncle crept in, and thoughts about that crazy scrapbook. I listened to as many noises as I could to try to make a silence in my head.

On Saturday afternoon, I was lying on my bed looking at the scrapbook, when the doorbell rang. I didn't care who it was. Someone selling cookies or trying to convert us to a different religion would have been great. But the buzzing was followed by my grandmother's excited voice.

"Felix! Won't you come in? Ethan! Felix is here!" This was the best noise I had heard all weekend.

I ran downstairs, slipping a little in my socks. Felix's eyes were red around the edges, like he had been crying. I knew if I asked him he would talk for an hour about allergies and asthma and any other excuse he could come up with.

"Hey," I said, "what's going on?" I thought Daron had been getting better, but in the movies that was always when people got worse.

Felix looked at me, and he stood up so straight he was almost as tall as I was. "Come outside," he said.

I didn't have shoes on, but Felix was insistent.

"Come on!"

We stepped outside. The concrete stair was rough under my socks, and the wind blew up my pants legs and through my sweatshirt.

"Something happened," Felix said.

"Okay."

"One of Daron's friends called and said they found out why Diego didn't come that night. They said somebody *told* him not to come. Do you know who they think told him?"

I didn't answer.

"Daron showed me this," Felix said. From his jeans pocket, he pulled out a damp, wrinkled piece of paper. I recognized my moon chart, the one I left in the pocket of Daron's sweatshirt the night we spied on him.

"I had to tell him how you borrowed his sweatshirt, how we heard them say about getting Diego. Now my brother thinks you was the one told Diego not to come.

You didn't tell him, did you? Just say you didn't, and I'll tell him he got it wrong."

I looked at Felix, and then I looked down at the ground. Across the street, a neighbor got into his car.

"Man!" Felix said, looking like he might cry. "You'll see."

Just then, my grandmother opened the door.

"Ethan, why aren't you wearing a coat? Or shoes! Honestly, Felix, I think your baby sister has more common sense than this boy."

Neither of us said anything. What did he mean, I'd see? Hadn't I seen enough?

"Well, don't just stand there," said my grandmother. "Either both of you come in, or Ethan, get some shoes and a coat."

Felix and I looked at each other. Then as usual, Felix found something to say.

"It was nice to see you, Mrs. Lowenstein. Bye."

I followed my grandmother inside as she droned on about how sometimes a person needed to think about what was logical, like wearing shoes.

As if anything in my life was logical.

It wasn't logical that I had thrown pebbles at Alex Krashevsky and ended up in an old-people world of cottage cheese and coupons.

It wasn't logical that I liked Sharita, or that she had gotten so angry when I told her about the pebbles, or that now she wanted me to help her organize a Hungry for Music concert.

It wasn't logical that because I protected Diego from getting hurt, Daron got hurt instead. And now that Daron was better, it wasn't logical that I had to lose my friendship with Felix because of what I did.

And my soon-to-be-divorced parents were the least logical of all.

16

I hadn't thought it was possible for school to get any lonelier, but as usual these days, I was wrong. All week, Felix and Daron waited outside for me as usual, so none of the adults would suspect something was up. But Felix had stopped talking to me, and Daron had never said much to begin with, and the quiet was hard to take. I started walking a few paces behind them so it wouldn't be as obvious that we weren't talking, but watching their matching blue backpacks — Daron's up about six inches higher than Felix's — was depressing in a different way.

And then there was Diego. It seemed like I should talk to him about what happened to Daron, but it was hard to find a time when we weren't in class or when José and Johnny weren't around. When I finally got to talk to him, Thursday after Social Studies, it wasn't much of a conversation.

"Hey, Diego," I said.

"Hey."

Long pause.

Think, Ethan. Say something.

"Hey, so, remember when I told you about that night?" I said. "About how if you went someplace, it might not be good, and then you didn't go? Well, there's this other guy — you might know him already, or at least somebody you know knows somebody he knows —"

"Ethan. Settle."

He was right. I sounded like an Amtrak train derailing off track at a million miles an hour. I sounded like Felix.

"Well, this guy, my neighbor, he got hurt pretty bad," I said.

Diego and I looked at each other.

Finally he said, "And I'm supposed to make him better?" He wiggled his fingers like someone casting a spell. "Doctor Diego to the rescue!"

"No, but —"

"Then I'm supposed to put somebody in a time-out chair? Tell a guy with a gun that widdle Da-won got his feelings hurt?"

So he did know Daron.

"No, I just —"

"E-man, if I come to Maple Sugarland someday, I'm not gonna know how things work up there, and I'll let you orient me around. So let me do the same for you. You keep your mouth shut, I keep my mouth shut, Daron Taylor keeps his mouth shut. That's how things work around here."

"But —"

Diego shook his head. "My mouth is shut. Daron Taylor's mouth is shut. And somebody's mouth is still open. Any idea whose it could be?"

I looked around. The hall was emptying out, and I still had to get downstairs to the band room.

Finally I shook my head.

⟨⟨⟨   ⟩⟩⟩

By Friday morning I knew what I had to do. Saying I was sorry would be the only way to prove I wasn't the same idiot kid who came here from Maple Heights in September. I knew I wasn't wrong to protect Diego, but I had to tell them that it was stupid for me to get involved with stuff I didn't know about. I just hoped they would forgive me.

While I ate my cereal I looked out the window at the Taylors' house, which looked eerily quiet.

The silence was interrupted by a big white truck with "Gulliver's Movers" written across the trailer. It turned onto our street and stopped in front of the Taylors' house.

Then, before I realized what was happening, two men climbed out of the truck and rang the doorbell. Mr. Taylor stepped outside. Then a car pulled up and a woman got out. Felix and Daron's aunt, maybe? Then Felix, Daron, and Kameka were out of the house and into her car and down the street before I had finished my corn flakes. The two moving guys went into and out of the house, carrying mattresses and bed frames.

I kicked the spindly wooden legs of my chair. Was that what Felix had meant when he said "You'll see" — that I'd see when I woke up and Gulliver's Movers was outside their house? After the dining room table was carried out of the Taylors' front door, my grandmother came into the kitchen. She put her hand on my shoulder, which didn't bother me as much as I would have thought.

"Where are they going?" I asked. I wanted to add, *And why didn't anyone tell me?* But I didn't want to sound like a baby.

"Didn't Felix tell you?" she said.

"No."

"What a funny child. They're moving out to Prince George's County, to be closer to Mrs. Taylor. I guess a good opportunity came along and they just took it."

When I didn't answer, my grandmother added, "He must be so disappointed to be leaving. It's so unlike that boy not to say anything."

After a minute, she cleared the cereal box, orange juice, and dirty dishes I had left on the table, and she wiped off the brown and white tablecloth with a sponge.

The two moving guys were handing chairs to a third guy, who was standing behind the truck and loading them in. I was only a year old when our family moved to the house in Maple Heights, but Margo remembered the townhouse where we lived before.

"That's the second family from our block this year," my grandmother was saying, "and Mr. Taylor said the Alsbrooks are thinking of going too. They say the schools are better in the suburbs. That seems to be the thing to do for middle-class black families these days."

"But — "

How could they have left without telling me? Before I could say I was sorry?

My grandfather came downstairs then, wearing a T-shirt and boxer shorts plus his Medic-Alert necklace and a giant black plastic wristwatch.

"What is this, some kind of peep show?" he said.

We didn't answer.

"If we're not inviting the neighbors in, could somebody *close the goll darn curtains!*" He waved his arms around but didn't do anything to cover up.

As my grandmother closed the curtains, my grandfather asked, "And what's he still doing here?"

"He got a little off-schedule this morning," my grandmother answered. "He didn't know the Taylors were leaving."

"Oh," said my grandfather. "That explains how you might not have noticed that school started, what, ten minutes ago?"

"Five minutes ago," I said.

"If I were you," said my grandfather, "I would hope the folks at school are as unobservant as you are this morning and get yourself over there before they notice you're missing."

Five minutes later I had located some socks, half-brushed my teeth, and made it outside, where the moving guys were struggling to get a sofa through the door.

Our block looked different with the Taylors on their way out. I saw a broken bottle near the curb, and across the street, one of the neighbors was wearing a long winter coat over an even longer bathrobe, sweeping her sidewalk. Next door, a much younger lady was getting into her car with a briefcase.

At school, the attendance monitor, an older African-American woman in a pink jogging suit, was sitting at a table just inside the door.

"Can I help you?" she said, sounding bored.

"Uh, I'm Ethan Oppenheimer."

"I didn't ask your name, I asked if I could help you," she said.

Oh.

"Well, I just need to go to class."

"If you *need* to go to class, why are you coming in here" — she looked at her watch — "twenty-three minutes late?"

"Uh, something unexpected came up," I said. That was true. "It won't happen again." Too true. Felix and Daron could only move away once.

"It better not happen again," she said. She paused. "Just because I see you with Miss Williams in the halls, I'm not about to let a boy with your future start adopting her patterns of attendance."

When had she seen me with Sharita in the halls? Who put her in charge of my "patterns of attendance"? What did she know about my future? And, most importantly, would she let me go to first period?

I spent the rest of first period in Room 110, copying over and over a long paragraph about why punctuality was important for my educational future. The girl behind me had a bag of powerfully scented nacho cheese Doritos under her notebook. Whenever the monitor went to the other side of the room, she took out a Dorito without crinkling the bag too much and chewed it as quietly as anyone can chew a Dorito.

By the time I had copied the paragraph three times, I could think about other stuff while copying. Like how I was starving for a Dorito. And what happened to all the kids who had etched their initials into the desk. And how

Felix and Daron were leaving, two more in the long list of people who had disappeared from my life. It wasn't fair. I was the kid in transit. Why couldn't everyone else stay put?

This was my first time being late to school, so I only had to copy the paragraph ten times, but even writing fast I only made it through eight and a half times before the bell rang for second period. One and a half paragraphs to copy that night at home. I mean, at my grandparents' house.

17

In a small metal box, my grandmother kept a file of index cards on everybody she knew. She wrote down their addresses and phone numbers, plus their birthdays and their kids' names, and if they had died. I once asked her why she kept people's index cards after they died.

"It's in case we outlive everybody we know," my grandfather answered. "If you don't save the dead people's cards, someday your card might be rattling around in there by itself."

My grandmother waved a dishtowel at him. "Ira, don't be ridiculous, there's no card in there for us. Like I'm going to write us a letter and forget where we live!"

Later, I had checked. My grandparents didn't have a card for themselves, but they had one for my family. It didn't mention my dad's apartment, like he had stopped existing when he moved out, but it did have Margo's address and phone number at college, even her e-mail address. It was probably the first e-mail address my grand-mother ever wrote down, because the @ symbol was back-wards.

I also found Felix and Daron's new information and copied it onto the back of a bright blue flyer advertising the winter band concert. My grandmother has loopy, old-fashioned handwriting, so I wrote down my three best guesses about the house number and the exact spelling of the street. The town, I could read clearly, was Clinton, Maryland, but I had no idea where that was.

I'm sure that if my grandfather ever had to drive me to Clinton, Maryland, he would complain the whole way about how far it was, how kids used to play with the other kids on their block, how if somebody moved you wrote them a letter maybe, but you didn't demand that adults who had better things to do drive you to another state so you could play stickball and tell bathroom jokes. So, even if he was willing to drive me to Prince George's County, I wasn't willing to sit through that speech. Besides, Sharita could take the bus by herself to the library; why couldn't I take the bus to Maryland?

I logged onto the Metro website and got bus directions during my lunch one day when the school librarian wasn't paying attention. (I also tried checking my email for about the fifth time since I'd arrived, but access was still denied.) My plan was to leave school early the next Friday and get

172

to Felix and Daron's house around the time they were getting home from school. I figured I could apologize in fifteen minutes or less. I would call my grandparents and say I had stayed after school for an emergency last-minute band rehearsal. Then I would see if Mr. Taylor could drive me home. Maybe I'd ask him to drop me off at the end of the block in case my grandparents were watching. My plan was as tight as an old margarine container.

⟨⟨⟨   ⟩⟩⟩

On Friday, I left school after sixth period. Not being popular had its advantages — no one even asked where I was going.

To get to Clinton, I had to take a bus, a Metro train, and then another bus. The last time I had ridden a Metro train was when my family went to the Air and Space Museum when I was seven. Of course, trains didn't run near the part of the city where my grandparents lived.

On Georgia Avenue, in a glass shelter across from the basketball court, I waited for a bus. And waited. I had seen lots of kids standing there, waiting to take the bus home. Now I was practically a city kid too. Or would be, when the bus came.

When a second bus went by in the opposite direction, I had a sudden and important question. Which way was

Maryland? Feeling like an idiot, I asked the driver of the next bus that pulled up.

"You need to go across the street and catch that other bus," he told me, pointing.

"Thanks." I tried to sound like I caught buses all the time.

Across the street, I had to wait another fifteen minutes. Seventh period was half over, and I was less than a block from school. Prince George's County seemed very far away.

Finally a bus pulled up. The fare was a dollar and twenty cents — I was proud I had looked that up ahead of time. I had packed two dollar bills, a quarter, a dime, and a nickel. I slid one of the dollar bills through the feeder, dropped the quarter into the slot, and waited for my change.

The driver looked at me. She was younger than the other driver, but not as friendly looking.

"You need a transfer?" she said.

"Oh, yeah. Thanks."

She handed me the transfer and stared at me.

"You need something else?"

"Uh, just my change. I put in five cents extra."

She stared at me harder, blinking slowly. It felt like the passengers, the ones in the sideways-facing seats looking out the window, were laughing at me. "You don't get no change on the bus," she said. She pointed to a sign on the fare box that said *Operator does not make change.*

"But I already — "

"I don't got time to argue with you. Next time, if the fare's a dollar and twenty cents, you put in a dollar twenty and you don't gotta worry about it. This time, you find a seat or get off the bus."

I shuffled back toward a seat, trying to avoid looking at anyone directly. No one paid attention to me except a little girl standing backwards on the seat in front of me, who stared at me with a serious expression. I half-waved hello, but she kept staring. A guy across the aisle had his iPod turned up loud enough that I could hear the bass.

We passed Wash-N-Glo Laundry, Joe's Chicken Shack, and Quik Express. (We sat for an especially long time in front of Quik Express.) For a while, the business names were in Spanish: L. J. Empañadas, Mimi's Salón. Then we began passing stone churches and big brick houses with nobody outside. I wondered who lived there, if it was black people or Spanish people or no people at all.

I looked at my watch: 3:11. Shouldn't I be on the train by now? I had planned to use this time to figure out what to say to Felix and Daron, but instead I was putting all my energy into getting there. And I wasn't even doing that right. My stomach felt sick. I had asked that first driver how to get to Maryland — but first I needed to get to the

Georgia Avenue-Petworth Metro station. Where was I going?

I stood up and said "excuse me" to the woman next to me. I held onto the tops of seats to keep my balance as I walked to the front of the bus.

When I reached the driver, I said, "Excuse me," again, and my voice sounded like a six-year-old's.

But the driver heard me.

"Yes?"

"I was — " Now my voice was cracking. "I need to go to the Georgia Avenue-Petworth station," I said.

The driver laughed like she lived for moments like these. Light reflected off gold fillings in the back of her mouth.

"And you just realized *now* that you're on the wrong bus?"

"Yeah," I said. I didn't tell her that I hadn't realized it for sure.

"Well, this bus goes to Silver Spring. That's what it says on the front. Might as well get off there and catch the Metro."

I was angry at her for laughing, but also grateful she was going to deliver me to a Metro stop. At Silver Spring, everyone got off the bus. The little girl in front of me waved goodbye, and I waved back. Her mother gave me a dirty look.

But I was in Maryland! I walked around the outside of the station until I found the ticket machines. A man in a Metro uniform was trying to un-jam a fare card, and I got up my courage and asked him how to get to Branch Avenue. He looked at me like I had asked where to board the space shuttle.

"Branch Avenue?" he said. "You go downtown to Metro Center and switch to the Green Line. You sure you want Branch Avenue?"

"Well, just to get a bus," I said.

His eyebrows went up. Was it because I was young, or white, or both?

"Your parents know you're going to Branch Avenue?"

"My parents are in Pennsylvania," I said, hoping it sounded like they were together in one house.

He sighed. "Okay, then, see that platform?"

He pointed to an area where signs said *Shady Grove* and *Glenmont.*

"Go up there, turn right, and walk down to the end. You get off at Metro Center, and look for somebody with this uniform. Ask them how to get to Branch Avenue."

"Okay," I said, nodding. "Thanks."

"Try to get home before dark," he added, turning back to the jammed machine.

That didn't sound good. I was hoping to see Felix and Daron and get home before my grandparents even noticed anything unusual. I reached into my pocket for the transfer, but it wasn't there. I searched all of my pants pockets and then turned back to the Metro guy.

"Um, one other question," I said to his back.

He had the whole front of the machine swung open and was jiggling something inside. He turned around.

"Um, how much does it cost? To Branch Avenue?"

"Two-twenty," he said.

"Okay, thanks," I said, trying to sound casual.

But I was panicking. I didn't have enough money to get there, and I would be stuck forever at the Silver Spring Metro station. It was 3:37. How long before my grandparents would call school? And what would they do when they found me? I couldn't blame them if they were sick of me, if this was the last straw, but where else could I go? My mom didn't want me home, my dad obviously didn't care, and I couldn't go to California and live with Margo in her dorm. I knew better than to think any of my "friends" in Maple Heights would actually help when I needed them.

Straight ahead was a green bench that was missing one of its planks. I slumped down on it to think.

18

Most of the people at the station were women, some with little kids. A bald, wrinkled man was fast asleep on a bench nearby, and further down I saw another man sifting through a garbage can. I didn't belong here, more than I had ever not-belonged in D.C.

I'd have to call my grandparents. The nice guy fixing the fare card machine had left, and the station manager refused to give me change for my dollar bill. But a woman carrying two shopping bags filled with blankets overheard our conversation and gave me two quarters and five dimes.

I had to wait at the pay phone while a woman with a lot of makeup cursed at someone on the other end.

"Listen, I *know* whose turn it is!" she was saying. "You don't have to tell *me* whose turn it is! All I'm saying is — "

Pause.

"You don't interrupt me! I'm saying he waited two hours for you on Saturday, two *hours* with his little face against that window, and I ain't gonna keep making excuses for you. You want excuses, you gonna have to come up with them yourself, 'cause that's it for me."

She slammed down the phone and turned around quickly. Her makeup was streaked. I stepped aside and let her storm past. Is that what it would have been like if my parents had split up when Margo and I were younger? It was hard to imagine my mom screaming into a pay phone, or my dad letting me wait next to a window for two hours, but I wondered.

I reached into my pocket, but instead of grabbing my change, I pulled out the slip of paper with Felix and Daron's address — which also had their phone number on it. If I was going to be in huge trouble anyway, maybe I should at least try to apologize to Felix. Before I could change my mind, I put money into the pay phone and dialed the Taylors' number.

I heard the phone ring once, twice, three times, then Felix's voice said, "Hello?" He sounded small and far away. I had never talked to him on the phone before.

"Hi, Felix?" I said. "I know you don't want to talk to me, but please don't hang up. I'm at a pay phone, and if you hang up I'm stuck here without a way home."

"Who *is* this?" he said, like he wasn't sure if I was a real person or a prank caller.

"It's Ethan. From D.C. But I'm at the Silver Spring Metro station. I wanted to say I'm sorry."

I hoped no one was behind me waiting to use the phone, listening the way I was with the woman in front of me, but I didn't turn around to look.

"You're in Silver Spring, Maryland?"

"Yeah," I explained. "I took a bus from school. I was going to take the Metro and then this other bus to your house, but I lost my transfer, and I don't have money for another fare."

"You were coming to my house?" Felix asked.

"Well, I wanted to, so I could apologize and everything. But I'm sort of stuck here."

"Hold on."

I heard the receiver bang against something, and then Felix yelling, "Dad! Dad!"

I worried we might get cut off. How much time would the pay phone give me? Finally, Felix came back on.

"My dad said we'll come get you, you should stand in front of the sign that says — " He laughed.

"Where?"

"The sign that says 'Kiss and Ride'!"

"For real?"

"Yeah, but we're just riding. No kissing."

"Okay."

"My dad will pull up in the car, and you'll eat dinner at

our house, and it's spaghetti night, and my dad said to ask if your grandparents know you're here."

I didn't answer.

"Ethan? You still there?"

"Um, I guess my grandparents don't exactly know yet," I said. "It sort of took longer to get here than I thought it would."

"Okay, well, bye. Don't forget, 'Kiss and Ride.'"

"Thanks," I said, but he had already hung up.

I walked around to the Kiss and Ride sign, which was near where I got off the bus. The bald guy was still asleep on the bench. I leaned against the bus shelter and tried to remember what kind of car Mr. Taylor drove.

Every time a car pulled up, I leaned forward to look at the driver, until somebody gave me a nasty look, like why was I looking in their car? It took a long time for Mr. Taylor and Felix to come. When they pulled up, Felix was in the front seat, and he didn't turn around to say hi.

"Thanks for picking me up," I said as I got in.

Whatever my grandparents decided to do with me, it wouldn't hurt for Mr. Taylor to mention that at least I had good manners.

"You're welcome," said Mr. Taylor, glancing at me in the rear-view mirror. "Before we left the house, I called your grandparents so they wouldn't worry."

"Thanks," I said, as if I had been planning to do that myself.

"They sounded pretty worried," he added.

"Yeah, I guess it took me a little while to get out here," I said.

"Uh huh," said Mr. Taylor, but something in his "uh huh" made me think he'd be saying more if I were one of his kids. Felix looked at me and smiled, shaking his head like he couldn't believe I got here. I was glad I couldn't see Mr. Taylor's face from the back seat.

"You'll stay over at our house tonight, and your grandfather will come pick you up in the morning," Mr. Taylor said.

Stay over? I was expecting to get creamed, and instead I got invited to a sleepover?

Felix still hadn't said anything. I could see the tops of his ears wiggling, though. He had gotten better at it.

"Really?" I said. "I mean, that's very nice of you."

"Uh huh," Mr. Taylor said again. "Tell you the truth, if I were you, I'd put off going home as long as I could."

"What do you mean?" I said.

"I lived next door to your grandmother seventeen years, and the only time she sounded as mad as she did on the phone was when the paper boy tracked fresh tar on her steps."

Oh.

When we got to the Taylors' Mr. Taylor parked in a big garage and we all went inside. A hallway was filled with boxes. The house was bigger than their old one, and it smelled like new wood and new paint. If living in my grandparents' house was like stepping back into the past, this house was like looking into the future: clean and bright. It felt like a place where a person could start over.

We walked straight to the kitchen, where Daron was setting the table and Kameka was tearing up peppers for a salad.

"What'd you do — drive to Japan?" Daron said. He looked fine, like himself, but when I looked closely I could still see a scar on his chin.

"Nice way to say hello to a guest," Mr. Taylor said.

"Hi," Daron said to me. "Felix, you gonna give him a tour?"

Felix shrugged. This was the longest I had ever been around Felix without him talking.

"Give him a five-minute tour," Daron said. "Kameka's gotta finish the salad."

Felix looked like he was weighing his options. Then he waved his arm wildly in a big circle, which seemed to mean I should follow him.

We ran down the hall, and Felix gestured to a closet near where we came in. He pantomimed taking off a coat and backpack and throwing them into the closet. When I

184

hesitated, he pointed to his watch. That's when I understood this was going to be a true five-minute tour.

I threw my coat and backpack in the closet. He pointed at the kitchen and pantomimed shoveling food in his face. Then he pointed at the empty living room and moved his hand around like a puppet while mouthing "blah, blah, blah." Then he pointed upstairs.

I followed him up a long staircase made of light, shiny wood. The staircase was so long it had a landing in the middle, which had boxes piled along one side. The house could have been in the new development near Maple Heights Mall.

At the top of the steps, Felix turned and sat down. He slid down two stairs on his butt, then he grinned at me and swooped his hand downward, showing how far he could slide.

"Why aren't you saying anything?" I asked, but he was standing up again, motioning for me to hurry up and follow him.

He showed me his room and Daron's room, which were connected by a small bathroom. He pointed to where a bathtub would be and moved his hands like he was sprinkling water over his head. No tub, only a shower. That was cool.

We walked past the door to Kameka's room (more "blah, blah, blah" from his puppet hand) and took a quick look at Mr. Taylor's room, which had its own bathroom with a tub. Then he looked at his watch, turned, and ran toward the stairs.

I ran after him, back through the hallway, past the kitchen, and down another staircase to the basement. He turned the light on and stood in the middle of the room with his arms open wide.

I looked around while Felix waited for me to say something. The room was empty, with a concrete-type floor and boxes stacked along the walls. It would be a good room for a PlayStation.

"It looks good," I said.

Felix jumped toward the wall and held an imaginary pool cue, which he aimed at an imaginary cue ball. He took an imaginary shot and raised his fist in the air, mouthing "Yes!"

"Uh, Felix?" He looked at me. "Why are we doing this tour in pantomime?"

Felix folded his arms across his chest and wrinkled his face into a funny expression. Then he sighed.

"See, I wanted to show you the tour, 'cause you're the first friend that's ever been to our house," he said. "But I'm still mad at you for what you did to Daron, so I'm still not talking to you. Except on the phone before. And right now."

I had never had so much fun with someone who wasn't

talking to me. I was trying to figure out how to answer when Daron's voice came from the top of the stairs.

"Yo, Felix! Bring the tour bus up to dinner!"

I followed Felix up the stairs.

"It wasn't a tour *bus*," he told Daron. "I'd like to see how you think we're getting a *bus* down to the basement."

"I take a bus to pre-K," Kameka announced.

"Yeah, we all take a school bus now," Felix told me.

"But my bus is just for pre-K and kindergarten," Kameka explained. "We sing songs. Want to hear 'The Wheels on the Bus'?"

"Sugar, let the boy get some food first," Mr. Taylor said. Then, to me, "That girl knows more verses to 'The Wheels on the Bus' than you'd believe. You'd better get some food in you."

"Thanks," I said.

I was starving. Six o'clock dinner felt late to me now. Fortunately, there was plenty of food, all of it for people under sixty-five: spaghetti and meatballs, garlic bread, and a huge salad with three colors of peppers.

"I hope you understand it's nothing fancy," Mr. Taylor said. "Next time maybe you'll call first, and we'll have time to cook something up."

"No, this is great," I said. "Thanks for having me."

"Ooh, I bet I know what's for dessert!" Felix said, scooping a mountain of spaghetti onto his plate.

"Nothing for anybody who doesn't eat his salad," Mr. Taylor said.

"I'm eating my salad!" Kameka said. "Red peppers and yellow peppers and green peppers, and every color pepper but I'm not eating cherry tomatoes!"

"There ain't no — aren't any — cherry tomatoes in there," Daron told her.

"I don't care," said Kameka.

At that moment, the Taylors felt like the most normal family on earth, even more normal than the families in cell phone commercials who stayed all connected and happy. And a million times more normal than my family. Chewing my meatball, I felt no need to go back to Maple Heights or Tillerman Avenue or anyplace else. If they would have adopted me, I would have moved in with the Taylors forever.

19

After dinner, Daron and Kameka cleared the table and Felix and I rinsed the dishes and put them in the dish-washer. A car horn honked outside.

"See you later!" Daron called.

"Ten-thirty," Mr. Taylor said.

"Daron's going back to the high school for a basketball game," Felix told me.

Except for his explanation in the basement, that was the first thing he had said directly to me. I thought I'd ask him a question, to see if he would keep going.

"What's your new school like?"

"Pretty good. But it's hard. They want us to read all these books." I handed him Kameka's cup, which was decorated with SpongeBob SquarePants.

"Yeah, my school in Pennsylvania was like that."

"So why'd you leave there anyway?"

"Your dad didn't tell you?"

"No, he made it like a big secret, so we thought you didn't want anyone to know. We decided you were probably an ex-con."

I wasn't sure if that was a compliment.

"So are you going to tell me?" Felix splashed me with some water.

"That depends," I said.

I flicked some water in his direction, in case he had splashed me on purpose.

"Hey, what'd you do that for?"

He splashed back, definitely not by accident. I picked up a sponge and used it to fling more water. Felix laughed, closer to a shriek.

His dad called from the living room, "Boys? Everything okay in there?"

"We're fine," Felix said, motioning me to stop. Then he said, "Hey, are you scared of the dark?"

"No." What did he think — I was five?

"Good!" he said. He loaded the last plate into the dishwasher and clicked it shut. "Follow me!"

He led me down the basement stairs again, but this time, when he got to the bottom, he pulled a flashlight down from the wall and shut off the light.

The darkness made me think about ice cream. When I was little, we would lose power at least once every summer, and my family would sit around in the dark and eat all the ice cream from the freezer before it melted. Eventually the power company put in better lines and we stopped losing our electricity so often.

"Scared yet?" Felix said.

"No."

"How about . . ." He switched on the flashlight under his chin, lighting up his face like a crazy jack-o-lantern. "Now?!"

I jumped back, and Felix laughed, a fake-evil, fake-scary laugh, "Bwa-ha-ha-ha!"

I laughed a little too.

"I think coming down here is like camping," he said, using the flashlight like a microphone. "Even though I've technically never been camping. Have you?"

"Well, when I was a kid, I used to go to this day camp, and every summer we had a sleepover in tents or whatever. So I guess that was like camping," I said.

"What did you do?"

"Not much. We looked for wood to make a fire, and we made s'mores."

That camp had been hot and not very fun. We ate sticky Popsicles that attracted a lot of bugs.

"What's s'mores?" Felix wanted to know.

"You roast marshmallows over a fire, and make a sandwich with them and graham crackers and Hershey bars."

"Wow, if I could have s'mores, I'd never eat anything else," Felix said.

"Yeah, they're good."

He pointed with his flashlight to a corner of the basement.

"Okay, so over here's the campfire, so we sit there, and that's where we keep the marshmallows and s'mores stuff."

"Okay." I felt kind of ridiculous, like we were back in third grade, but it was okay. Back in third grade, my parents still lived together, and I hadn't yet done anything horribly stupid.

"So why did you come here?" Felix was still using the flashlight to make his face look like a Halloween creature. When it was my turn to talk, he shone the flashlight in my face.

"Here like Washington, or here like your house?"

"Oh yeah!" Felix said. "You never said why you came to Washington! Was it to be part of the witness protection program? Me and Daron saw a special on TV about the witness protection program, and I said, 'That sounds like Ethan!'"

"I don't think people in the witness protection program go live with their grandparents, usually. I think they have to go where nobody knows them."

Felix sighed.

"That's what Daron said."

I took a deep breath.

"I — I'm sorry. I feel bad about what happened to Daron."

Felix talked directly into the flashlight, in a fake-deep monotone voice.

"I-ac-cept-your-a-polo-geeeeee," he said. "You-do-not-need-to-feel-baaaad."

"Well," I didn't want to talk him into hating me again, but I was confused. "But — why? For a while I thought you were never going to talk to me again."

"That-was-be-fore-you-came-here-to-vi-sit," he said into the flashlight.

"Can you stop talking like an alien?"

"Not-talking-like-aliiiien. Talking-like-com-pooterized-ro-bot."

"Whatever," I said. "Why did coming here make a dif-ference?"

"I-was-mad-'cause-you-not-know-what-you-did-was-stoooo-pid. You-came-far-a-way-to-say-you-were-sorrrrr-y."

"Do you think Daron will stop being mad at me too?"

Felix sat up.

"Daron wasn't mad to start with," he said in a normal voice.

"He wasn't?"

"He said you were just a naïve kid from the suburbs."

Felix tried to balance the flashlight on his head. "He said what you did made sense to you."

"Oh."

He was right, of course. I hadn't even been smart enough to know not to spy on a gang while they figured out some mess with their drugs or whatever. I should have been more scared that night.

Felix moved the flashlight back in front of his mouth like a microphone. He resumed the annoying robot voice.

"So-if-you-not-part-of-witness-protection-proh-gram, whyyyy-you-come-to-Wash-ing-ton?"

It was only fair to tell him. "It was because of some stupid stuff I did. Only one other person down here even knows about it."

"Can-I-tell-Daaaaron?" he asked. "I-don't-keep-secrets-from-my-bro-ther."

"I guess." I took a deep breath and began, "So there was this kid named Alex."

I told him the whole story, and for once he didn't interrupt me with questions. Afterwards he was quiet. Maybe he would never talk to me again, but as long as he didn't make me sleep on the lawn, I wouldn't be worse off than before I came. I waited.

After a while, he said, "That's just like what happened to Daron."

It was?

"You know, other kids try to get you to do something stupid, and you're the one that ends up getting beat up or having to move away or whatever."

"Yeah, maybe," I said. "I didn't think I was even capable of being that stupid."

"I knew Daron was capable of being stupid," Felix said, "but I didn't think he'd do it."

"Yeah." I leaned back against the wall, felt the unfinished concrete floor under my hands. "Did you ever find out what those guys were doing that night we spied on Daron?"

Felix shone the flashlight in my eyes.

"Stop it!"

"Sorry."

He shone it up at the ceiling instead. We looked up at a bright circle surrounded by smaller circles of different widths.

"Drugs," he said. "What else? Daron said they like to have junior high kids do their running for them, 'cause it's no big deal if you get caught when you're younger."

"Man."

"Yeah."

Felix waved the flashlight around so it made a design on the ceiling.

"That drug stuff, you know, we always said we'd stay away from that. You know, 'cause that's what made those guys accidentally shoot our mom. Nobody would shoot my mom on purpose, they was just messed up from drugs."

I thought about my mom, alone in the big house in Maple Heights. I wished she could take me home and I could redo the last few months.

"So why did Daron do it? Was it for money?"

"No. What do you think, we're poor? Does this house look like it belongs to poor people?"

"No. Sorry."

"He said he did it 'cause he thought junior high kids were dumb. Daron wanted to hang out with high school kids."

"Oh."

"But they just treated him like dirt. Now he says it was better being with junior high kids, where he could treat them like dirt instead."

"So is he okay now?"

"Yeah, he's good. But in Maryland, ninth grade is part of high school, not junior high, so he gets to be in high school anyway. He's on the freshman basketball team, and this other club where they build rockets."

"Cool."

"Yeah. I wish we could build rockets!"

Mr. Taylor called from the top of the stairs, "Boys! Time to come up for bed."

196

"But Dad," Felix complained, "it's Friday, we don't got school tomorrow."

"We don't what?"

"We don't *have* school tomorrow," Felix corrected himself.

"No, but at least one of you has a very long day ahead of you with some unhappy grandparents."

Felix gave me a sympathetic look.

"But — "

"And if you don't want *both* of you having a very long day tomorrow, I'd suggest coming upstairs and brushing your teeth in the next two minutes. Ethan, you'll find an extra toothbrush next to the sink."

"Okay, okay, we're coming," Felix said.

With everything happening, I had forgotten about having to face my grandparents in the morning. I thought I would be up all night worrying. But curled up in a sleeping bag on Felix's floor was the best night's sleep I'd had in a long time.

20

My grandfather came at nine-thirty the next morning, while we were eating chocolate-chip pancakes. Kameka had spilled chocolate chips while she was "helping" earlier, and we had picked most of them up. But once in a while someone would move their foot and a chocolate chip would fly across the room.

"Hello, there," I heard my grandfather say to Mr. Taylor. "Thanks for keeping Ethan last night. My wife gets funny about me driving around after dark, ever since I had that problem with the cataracts. I hope he wasn't too much trouble."

I didn't know my grandfather didn't drive at night because of cataracts.

"No trouble at all," Mr. Taylor said. "Why don't you join us for some pancakes?"

"Thank you, I already ate," my grandfather said. "You

get to my age and you find yourself eating high-fiber cereal at an hour most decent folks aren't yet out of bed."

Mr. Taylor laughed. "I understand. I'll get Ethan."

"Good luck, man," Felix whispered to me. "If you make it home alive, I hope you can sleep over again."

"Me too," I whispered back. "Thanks for letting me stay here."

I thanked Mr. Taylor too, loud enough for my grandfather to hear. Even though I had skipped seventh period and come to Maryland without telling anyone, at least I had good enough manners to thank my host.

On the ride home, I kept glancing at my grandfather, wondering when he was going to tell me about my punishment. But he just kept driving, staring straight ahead.

The longer he was quiet, the more I was convinced they were going to send me away. He probably thought I had pajamas and a toothbrush with me, so why would we need to go back to Tillerman Avenue? I figured that when we got wherever we were going, he'd say something like, "Your grandmother is sorry she couldn't say goodbye."

But where were we going? Military school? I didn't know anything about military school, but I was sure the food would be worse than what we ate at my grandparents'. They probably mushed it together and let it get cold, so everyone got one blob of congealed, lumpy goop.

My grandfather stopped the car on a familiar-looking

street and opened his door. I was still thinking about the food at military school, wishing I had eaten more chocolate-chip pancakes at the Taylors'.

My grandfather looked at me.

"What are you waiting for — the butler to open your door?"

"No, sorry. Sir," I added, still thinking about military school.

"'Sir.' Hmmph," said my grandfather.

I slung my backpack over one shoulder, and slowly followed behind him up the steep hill.

"Kids," my grandfather said to no one in particular. "Act like they need a personal valet to escort them door to door. Act like walking a couple of blocks is the end of the universe. The way I see it, if you're going to spend four hours circling the block looking for a parking space and then park three blocks from home, why not park three blocks from home to begin with and use the four hours to get a start on walking?"

We turned onto Tillerman Avenue. I had never been so happy to see the clean little house, even if it wasn't as fancy as the Taylors' new place. I was tempted to throw my arms around my grandfather and give him a hug, but he wasn't the hugging type. Instead I thanked him for picking me up.

He grunted. "I got the easy job, picking you up. Your

grandmother got the job of figuring out what to do with you."

Uh oh.

When we got inside, my grandmother was standing right inside the front door.

"What took so long?" she said to my grandfather, and he repeated his theory about why it was better to park three blocks away than have to hunt for a spot.

"But there are spots right out front," she said.

She was blocking the hallway, and my grandfather and I stood in front of her, holding our jackets.

"You had us very worried," my grandmother told me.

"I know," I said. "I'm sorry — "

"Don't interrupt me. You had us very worried because your mother expects us to keep you out of trouble. Now it looks like we can't even keep track of what county you're in."

"I know. I didn't mean — "

"Stop interrupting your grandmother," my grandfather said. "This isn't Maple Heights, Pennsylvania, where a person can't get a word in edgewise. Your grandmother will let you talk when she's done."

My grandmother glared at him, like he wasn't any better than I was. He sat down on the bottom step, took off his shoes and socks, and bent over to examine a corn on his foot.

"Now, if you were our child," my grandmother said, waving her cleaning rag in my direction, "I can assure you that you would not sit down comfortably for at least a week, and even after that you'd feel it in your backside every time a city bus went by."

I had never seen my grandmother even swat a bug, but I believed her.

Like she was reading my mind, she said, "And if I ever hear of you trying anything like this again — even if you don't go out of state — I will consider that proof positive that modern child-raising methods are deficient, and I will personally make up for every spanking you ought to have got in your life. Is that clear?"

I nodded.

"For the interim, however, your grandfather and I are tired. We're not as young as we used to be, and we don't think it's worth getting your mother hysterical over a question of how you ought to be disciplined. So you, sir, can consider yourself a very lucky boy."

I couldn't remember the last time someone called me a boy (or lucky), but my butt tingled in gratitude. I thought back to the first day I stayed after school for an oboe lesson, and Felix asking if my grandparents would ever hit me. Now I knew the answer.

"So," my grandmother went on. "They're calling for

quite a bit of snow tonight, and you'll have plenty of opportunity to help shovel out the neighbors."

Was this it? I waited for her to continue, like I'd have to shovel with a toothbrush, or I'd have to do it naked except for a ball and chain around my ankle, but she didn't say anything else.

"Okay," I said, letting out my breath.

"And next time, I hope you'll ask before setting off to visit friends out of state."

"Oh, definitely," I said.

That night, I thought about playing "Let it snow, Let it snow, Let it snow" on the oboe, but I hummed it in my head instead.

The snow began during dinner on Sunday. No school tomorrow, I thought at first, but then I remembered that a snow day sitting around my grandparents' house — or shoveling out their neighbors — was not as exciting as a snow day in Maple Heights. Was it snowing in Maple Heights? Josh and Caleb and Tyler were probably instant-messaging right at that moment, making plans to go sledding on the hill behind Tyler's house. Tomorrow they'd sleep in and go sledding, then they'd go to Caleb's and order pizza and play video games for the rest of the day.

After dinner, I watched the local news with my grandparents — actually watched it, not just listened from upstairs. The newscasters were older-looking than I expected from their voices, and the women wore a lot of makeup.

"Can you believe this weather!" the female newscaster said, all fake-y, her voice as bright as her lipstick.

"Tell me about it," said one of the male newscasters. "Two inches on the ground already, and another *six* inches before it tapers off around midnight. I hope you've stocked up on bottled water!"

They laughed.

"I did, Bob, and all around the metropolitan area, people are still stocking up on essentials! Let's go to Lisa, who's at the Safeway in Bethesda."

Lisa was even more pink than the first newscaster. "Here at the Safeway on Old Georgetown Road, people are preparing in case they're stuck in the house tomorrow!" she said, catching a shopper by the elbow and jabbing a microphone under his chin. "Sir, what's the most important item you've got in your basket?"

The man had to bend down to talk into the microphone. "Well, that would be Fruit-by-the-Foot," he said. "We've got a three-year-old at home, and if he's missing his Fruit-by-the-Foot, our whole house is going to be unhappy."

My grandfather got up, picked up the remote control from the top of the TV, and shut it off.

"Fruit by the foot, my knee," he said. "I don't know

204

which is more ridiculous, parents running out in a snow-storm to buy their kid snacks, or people who think two inches of snow is a blizzard."

"At least their little boy wants fruit," my grandmother said. "At least they're not running out in the snow to buy junk food."

"Actually, Fruit-by-the-Foot is more like candy," I said. Finally my knowledge of processed food was useful for something.

"Really?" said my grandmother.

"Yeah," I said. "It comes in strips of weird colors, and you peel it off and eat it." I could almost taste the sticky sweetness of Rainbow Punch.

"Hmmph," said my grandfather. "Used to be, kids were lucky to get a piece of fruit off a tree. Now they send their parents out in a blizzard to buy them candy."

"Now, Ira, you said yourself it's not a blizzard," my grandmother pointed out.

"Well, it's enough that it wouldn't kill Ethan to go around tomorrow and see who on the block needs help with their sidewalks."

"That's true, it wouldn't kill him."

So that was how I spent my snow day. I shoveled four walks before lunch. In the afternoon, at the last house on the corner, I was halfway up the walk before I realized someone else was shoveling the steps. Someone wearing a pink winter coat. I turned to leave, but my shovel scraped against the ground and a girl about my age looked up at me.

"Hi," she said. "I know who you are."

She had about a million braids in her hair, and big, round eyeglasses with clear plastic frames.

"Uh, hi," I said.

"You're Ethan Oppenheim, right? You live with your grandparents up the street. I wondered if I would run into you here."

I had no idea who she was.

"Uh, Oppenheimer," I said. "Not to be rude or whatever — do I know you?"

"No, and I'm sorry for not introducing myself." She stuck out a hand wearing a turquoise and silver waterproof glove. "My name is Lynnette Hughes. I go to church with Sharita."

I was still puzzled.

"But you don't live . . . here?"

"No, my grandparents do. I was staying with them yesterday, me and my little sisters, and everybody figured since we've got the day off, we'll all just hang out here for today."

"Oh," I said. "But how do you . . . ?"

"Know who you are?" Lynnette said. "I was the one told Sharita all about you. Or some about you. I told her

206

your grandparents' last name, anyway. She described them to me, and I said, that has to be the couple across the street from my grandparents. Does your grandmother still bake that apple cake?"

"Uh, sometimes," I said.

I remembered her and Kameka baking apple cake when Daron got hurt. I had never liked apple cake. But, wait, Sharita had talked to her friend about me?

"Yeah," she said. "That's too bad it didn't work out with you and Sharita. But like I told Sharita, we're fourteen — how old are you?"

"Fourteen," I said.

Well, almost.

"And that's really too young to make a big commitment. Especially given Sharita's circumstances."

"Yeah," I said, like I knew what Sharita's circumstances were. Up the street, a car spun its wheels on the ice. Lynnette shook her head.

"Mm-mm-mm," she said, sounding more like a grandmother than a kid my age. "Well, I'm glad to see there's one person at her school who doesn't hold her family against her. The way she talks, you'd think the whole school was out to get her."

"Yeah," I said again.

A pause.

"Do you know her little niece?"

Lynnette practically shrieked, "Yes! Isn't she the cutest? Sharita is so in love with that little dollbaby. I tell her, though, I say, Reetie, there's time for those later. First you gotta get a college degree. Somebody's gotta make sure she don't end up like her sister."

"Uh huh."

"I mean, it's not fair to Jamil and Latasha, only seeing their momma when someone can drive them down to Alderson. I tell her, Reetie, not only don't you be getting in trouble, you don't even be hanging with people that might make somebody *think* you be getting in trouble."

I wasn't sure what Alderson was, but I had an idea.

"It sounds like you guys are good friends," I said.

"We look out for each other," Lynnette said. "Sometimes we meet at the library to study and stuff."

Had Lynnette been at the library that day of the stairwell kiss? Had they met up afterward and talked about me? I remembered Sharita's mouth against mine, the little gap where her lips were parted slightly. I was glad for my grandfather's big winter coat, the one my grandmother had insisted I wear for shoveling snow.

Lynnette pointed to the stairs. "I should get back to these."

"Yeah, I got more shoveling too," I said. "But it was nice meeting you."

"You too."

I shoveled two more walks and thought about what Lynnette had told me without actually telling me. Whatever Alderson was, I couldn't blame Sharita for not wanting to end up there, or with a baby. If I wanted to be her friend, I had to show her I was on the right track. We would try to raise a million dollars for Hungry for Music, and I would play the oboe better than I had ever played before.

〈〈〈　〉〉〉

It was almost five-thirty when I came inside, and my grandparents had already eaten. I wanted something processed, like a Hot Pocket, but healthy food was better than starving to death.

As I was standing with the refrigerator door open, my grandfather came up behind me. I expected a lecture about wasting energy, but he just waited for me to take out a Saran-wrapped plate of leftover casserole my grandmother had put aside for me.

"There's sauce in the butter dish," he said.

I looked over my shoulder, puzzled.

"In the what's-it-called, the plastic thing that says 'I can't believe it's not butter!' Not only is it not butter, it's some kind of orange sauce your grandmother likes to put on the chicken."

"Is it good?"

My grandfather shrugged. "You get older, you don't taste things the way you used to. You also don't understand why some people like their chicken to taste like oranges. But it's not bad."

The chicken was pale and forgotten-looking under the Saran wrap, even though it was recently cooked, so I decided to add the orange sauce. I heated everything up in the microwave, which was the Model T of microwave ovens. My grandfather poured himself some diluted apple juice in a Washington Redskins mug and sat across from me at the table while I ate.

After I finished, my grandfather stood up and peeked through the kitchen doorway like he was standing lookout.

Then he stage whispered to me, "Ethan! Something I gotta show you."

I was afraid of what it could be, like an old-person magic trick where he made his teeth disappear.

He got a serious look on his face and said, "If you're going to be living here, this is something you have to know."

He made sure I was watching, and he stood up and walked the two steps to the pantry.

"Now the first thing," he said, reaching up to the top shelf, "is you gotta move these out of the way."

He took down two bulky phone books, one at a time,

and put them on the table. "Then you move these out of the way." He took down a Hanukkah menorah, some Shabbat candlesticks, and a couple of boxes of candles. "Then — " he was far enough back in the cabinet that he couldn't see what he was doing but had to rummage around with his hand — "Aha! Then you bring *these* down."

He set down on the table a partially full package of double-stuff Oreos, bound together with a rubber band so the plastic covering was sticking out in every direction. Clearly, this had not been packaged by my grandmother.

"Well, what do you think?" His face was glowing like he had given me a puppy, a bicycle, and my parents' marriage back together all at once.

"Wow. I don't know what to say."

And I didn't. These were real Oreos, not the store brand. My grandfather nodded.

"Used to be, you couldn't ask for something much better than an Oreo. Then they started making them with double filling. Just goes to show you."

I waited for him to finish, but he didn't say anything else. After a minute, he took three Oreos from the bag and ate them over his cupped hand. He nudged the bag toward me, and I took some Oreos too, and we sat there like that for a while, chewing and swallowing. Just two guys and, finally, some regular-people food.

21

Back at school after the snowstorm, I couldn't wait to talk to Sharita. Now that I knew she had asked Lynnette about me, my hopes were climbing. I was writing a note to her in social studies — actually, drawing musical instruments that were eating junk food around the edges of the paper while I figured out what to say in the note.

I drew an arrow pointing to a tuba eating ice cream and was writing, "Get it? 'Hungry for Music'?" when another sheet of paper landed on my desk with a thwap. It was Diego's and my outline for the civil rights project, which Janeen was passing back. At the top Mr. Kirk had written, "Good start. Try to include some oral history. Find someone who lived here in 1968 and ask what they remember."

At dinner, I asked my grandparents about the riots.

"What do you need to know about that for?" my grandmother said. "I thought you already went to the library."

"We're doing oral history now," I said. "Was it, like, buildings burning down all over the place?"

My grandmother waved her hand.

"Who's ready for more sweet potatoes?" When my grandfather and I didn't answer, she looked at my plate. "Ethan, you've hardly touched your brisket."

I shrugged. "I'm not hungry." I couldn't remember ever not being hungry before, but it was true. The brisket was okay, not too dry, not too stringy, but it was hard to eat and think about riots at the same time.

"I never understood it," my grandfather said. "They blamed all the wrong people. Instead of taking their anger out on the people who left, the rioters took it out on the people who stayed. I guess they figured, why schlep to Silver Spring when we can destroy things right here on Fourteenth Street? Of course, that was before the Metro."

"What do you mean? Who didn't want to schlep to Silver Spring?" I said. This sounded like what I needed for my project, if I could get it to make sense.

"Don't worry about it," my grandmother said. "You've got enough to worry about."

My grandfather shook his head.

"I never did figure that out," he said. "Even your mother found a way to make it our fault."

"Ira, drop it already. She was barely a teenager."

My grandfather shrugged, but my mind was racing. If

213

riots broke out tomorrow and burned down buildings around the city, I would remember it long enough to tell my kids. I did some quick calculations: my mom had been fourteen at the time of the riots.

After dinner, without thinking about the phone bill or what I would say, I called home. I thought I would get the answering machine, but my mom answered on the first ring, like she was waiting for someone.

"Hello?"

"Hi."

"Ethan! How are you?"

She paused for me to answer. Before I messed everything up by saying how I was, I blurted out, "I'm doing a project on what happened in D.C. in 1968, the riots and stuff. I'm supposed to ask what you remember."

"What *I* remember?"

"Yeah, what Washington was like then."

I expected her to say she was busy, or on her way out the door, but instead she said, "This is for a project?"

"Yeah, for social studies."

"Hmm. When Margo had a social studies project, it usually meant I had to drive her somewhere."

"I guess I'm the easy kid," I said, expecting her to laugh. But she was quiet. "I can call back later — or, you know, if you don't want to talk about it or whatever — "

"No, I'll tell you what I remember," she said. "I'm just trying to think where to start."

As my mom talked, I could finally imagine her growing up in this house. I pictured her in elementary school, with pigtails and skinned knees, playing with her friends outside Tillerman Elementary. I imagined what it would be like to have the other white kids in school move away, one at a time, without knowing why.

"It was called 'blockbusting,'" she told me. "The city had certain sections for white people and certain sections for African Americans, only back then they were called 'colored.' A real estate agent would sell a house in a white section to an African-American family, then scare all the other white families around into selling their houses real cheap. Then the real estate agent would pump up the prices and sell at a big profit to African Americans. It was amazing how fast all those people got out of there once they thought their neighborhood was declining."

"But not Grandma and Grandpa," I said.

"No, not Grandma and Grandpa."

While we talked, I played with a thread that was unraveling from my shirt, near my wrist. The clothes from ValuBuy weren't holding up great, but I had grown half an inch and the shirt was almost too small anyway.

Then my mom and I started to talk at the same time:

"I don't understand — "

"It wasn't — "

"You go first," I told her.

"Well, my friends were moving away," she said. "I used to — well, you don't need to hear this."

"It kind of helps."

"Well," she said. "If it helps."

And then she told me about eating her lunch under the stairs, which I didn't mention were the same stairs where I sometimes ate my lunch, only people would purposely drop things on her head while she tried to eat. Kids used to trip her when she walked into the auditorium for an assembly. She once got in trouble for being late to class because she was scrubbing off nasty words someone wrote on her locker. Parker was nothing like Maple Heights Middle School even when my mom went there.

"Then there was this other world," she went on. "I belonged to this youth group at the synagogue where all the other kids lived west of Rock Creek Park. They looked at me a little funny too, like what was I doing living over where I did. But they were better than the kids at school."

"Yeah," I said. The thread hanging from my shirt was longer now, but I couldn't stop pulling it, like if I didn't focus on something here in real life, I might get totally sucked away into my mom's story.

"So in April 1968 we all went to Virginia for this Jewish youth conference, this big-deal weekend people had been planning all year. We left on a Thursday after school, and we were finishing up our dinner, singing the grace after meals, when we heard Martin Luther King, Jr., had been shot. Of course everyone was upset, naturally, but it wasn't until the next morning that we heard he had died, and that there was rioting in Washington."

I imagined what it would be like to hear about riots in Maple Heights while I was out of town. No way would I have stuck around any Jewish youth conference.

"The kids from west of the park were going crazy," she continued. "But they had different ideas about what was a dangerous 'riot' versus what was just drunk people outside making noise. But when they all lined up at a pay phone to call their parents, I thought I should call my parents too."

A long-distance call. I could almost hear my grandfather complaining about the phone rates.

"I couldn't reach them, which didn't worry me at first even though the conference ended early so we could all go home. But someone had brought a transistor radio, and as we got closer to Washington, we found out exactly where the riots were. And the thing was — " My mom paused. "The thing was, the riots were going on right outside my father's store."

I imagined my mom in a van, looking at everyone else

looking out the window because they didn't know what to say.

"So after that, I figured they were probably dead — I shouldn't be saying this to you, except you know it turned out okay."

"It's okay," I said.

"So when we finally got back to the city, there's this interminable delay until we could enter the city limits."

"Interminable delay" was one of my mom's favorite phrases when she was working on a big case or getting bad customer service in a store.

"There were policemen asking the driver all sorts of questions, and this one girl, Debbie Bloom, they made her open up her bag with all her personal items. She had been obnoxious to me the whole trip, so I didn't mind that. But they finally let us go on, and when we got to the synagogue, everyone else's parents were waiting for them."

"So how did you get home?" I said.

"Some girl's parents took me back to their house in Cleveland Park. Even without the riots, the idea of driving to my house was like driving to Mars, but at least they took me back to their house. A couple of hours later, my parents showed up, arguing over whose fault it was they had gotten the pick-up time wrong."

Typical.

"So . . . were you glad to see them?" I said. I wanted to

keep her on the phone, like just having her there might answer some of my questions.

My mom snorted, the way she used to snort when Margo or I asked if she could get off from work early or not have to go in on a weekend.

"Are you kidding?" she said, just like she used to.

But then she said, "I had thought they were dead. I was so angry at them for putting me through this I couldn't be happy to see them. And when my father went back to his store to clean up, I couldn't even acknowledge where he was. I figured, how could he go back there if he cared about us? But of course he didn't see it that way. Strength in our routines! You've probably heard him say that."

I had seen him live that, anyway, with his scheduled coupon-clipping and the six o'clock news. A few things were starting to make sense, like why Mom didn't get along great with her parents, and why my grandfather didn't talk about his pharmacy. I looked around Uncle Ed's bedroom, the time capsule, and I saw the scrapbook sitting on the desk.

I hesitated and then said, "You know, I found a box of your stuff in Uncle Ed's closet."

"Really?"

"Yeah, mostly report cards and junk, but there's this scrapbook from 1968. It has all these news articles and things I've been using for my social studies project."

"Really?" my mom said again. "I wondered what ever happened to that."

"It's here," I said. "But — it seems weird that you made a scrapbook like that. I mean, were other kids so obsessed with the news?"

My mom paused.

"I'm not sure 'news' is really the right word for something you're living in the middle of. People landing on the moon the following year, that was news. But the place you live going up in flames, that's not news, that's something else. I wouldn't expect you to understand."

And I didn't understand completely, but the place I lived, back home in Maple Heights, was disappearing in a different way, with Dad and Margo leaving, Mom "readjusting," and my friends bailing out on me. Maybe I understood more than my mom realized.

"So why did you make a scrapbook?" I asked her.

"It was something people did then," she said. "They saved ticket stubs and little things to remember certain parts of their lives. But I didn't get invited that many places that required tickets, and I wasn't sure I wanted to remember that much about my personal life. Those articles, those were things my brother was always talking about, so I thought maybe if I could understand those things better, it would help me understand my brother."

"Did it?"

My mom sighed. "Uncle Ed did a lot of things I'm not sure anyone will ever understand. But understanding what mattered to him, what he cared about, I guess that didn't hurt."

"What did he care about?" I asked.

"Oh, he had these ideas — he was going to re-create the Freedom Rides from the early '60s and get the whole country stirred up. He had a lot of crazy ideas."

Like me? I wondered. True, some of my crazy ideas (Hungry for Music concert) were better than others (that stupid day outside Maple Heights Middle School). But would anyone ever try to understand me and my crazy ideas?

"Why did you send me here?" I asked.

My mom's breathing was loud and steady, like one of those machines that pumps helium into balloons. You hear it pump and pump until you don't think the balloon will hold any more, and then it stops and the balloon is much stronger than a regular balloon, pulling your hand up to the sky.

"Your grandfather — " she said. "Oh, I'm sorry."

"What are you saying?"

"It was his idea. He thought it would be good for all of us, for you to spend some time with them in Washington. That I couldn't take care of you until I started taking care of myself. "

I tried to understand what my mom meant. So she hadn't sent me away just because of the rocks and Alex Krashevsky. My mom sent me away so she could cope with things, things like the fact that her family was falling apart. Part of me had suspected this, maybe, but I had never in a million years suspected that my grandparents wanted me to come. That they had suggested it! They knew I would mess up their coupon-clipping and who knew how many other routines, and they wanted me anyway.

"How are things working for you?" my mom asked.

I wanted to answer that what worked for me was being home with my parents and my sister like normal people. But the chances of that happening again were pretty much zero.

Life with my grandparents was not normal food-wise or technology-wise or just about any other-wise. But some of what they did, like eating dinner together and watching the news, seemed strangely normal, even if their evenings started much earlier than most people's. And the kids I knew who didn't torment me, Felix and Daron and Sharita and Diego, plus the other kids in jazz band and even Lynnette whose grandparents lived down the street — they weren't exactly what you would call normal, but they weren't the worst people in the world either.

"Ethan?"

I had forgotten to answer my mom's question.

"Yeah. I mean, yeah, I think things are working out more than I thought, too."

"Well, sweetie, good luck on your social studies project."

"Thanks. And good luck on, you know, whatever."

"Thanks."

After we hung up, I practiced the oboe for an hour and a half, and I finally understood what Mr. Harper meant when he said to put soul into music. Soul came from eating weird chicken with orange sauce and not minding that nobody else would ever eat that. Nobody else played jazz oboe, either, or lived a life that was quite so abnormal, but so what? Whose life was normal, anyway?

I put so much soul into my oboe-playing that night that it felt like Felix and Daron could hear me up in Maryland, and Sharita could hear me in Southeast, and Diego could hear me wherever he lived. Maybe people could even hear me in California, or in Old City, Philadelphia, or even in Maple Heights.

22

The Friday before our social studies projects were due, Mr. Kirk let us work on them in class, and I brought the scrapbook to show Diego. We had been doing a pretty good job of keeping our mouths shut around each other, but we had to finish the project. The scrapbook fit inside my backpack if I left it partly unzipped, so my grandparents didn't see it leave the house.

"Here," I said to Diego, after everyone had finished moving around to sit with their partners. "This is a scrapbook I found in my uncle's room. There's stuff here about the riots."

"Yeah? Let's see."

I turned the pages slowly, and we looked at all of the pictures and headlines. It was different from when I first came to D.C., before I had heard any of the street names. The paper was yellow and the people in the pictures had funny haircuts, but otherwise it wasn't hard to imagine that the riots happened, like, last month or last year.

"Man," said Diego, looking at the pictures. "Why was your cousin so into those riots? Was he psycho or something?"

"No, he wasn't psycho! First of all, he was my uncle, not my cousin." I didn't mention that my mom was the one who made the scrapbook.

Diego gave me a strange look. "Okay, okay. He still alive?"

"No, he — he died of a bad reaction to some medicine."

Diego grinned.

"Medicine or *med*icine?"

If by *med*icine he meant drugs, I had started to wonder the same thing. But I just looked at him.

"He's dead, okay?" I said.

"Okay."

We looked at a few more pages before Diego asked, "Were there riots in Pennsylvania? Where you lived?"

"Where I live? No!" It was hard to imagine rioters breaking windows at Blockbuster or Starbucks. Maple Heights Mall probably wasn't even built yet in 1968. Then I reconsidered. After all, we had learned that riots happened all over the country.

"Maybe there were riots in Philadelphia. I don't know. But we don't go into Philadelphia that much." *Even though my dad lives there now,* I thought but didn't say.

"You like the Phillies, though."

I remembered my dad teaching me how to keep score and explaining the infield fly rule. It was so hot that the sweat on his leg soaked through the paper bag of peanuts we had bought outside the stadium. And I remembered Diego convincing his friends not to beat me up because of my Phillies cap.

"Yeah, I like the Phillies."

"What would you do if there was riots here tomorrow? Would you stay here or go back to Log Cabin Lite?" he said.

I ignored the dig on Maple Heights.

"There aren't gonna be riots tomorrow," I said.

"How do you know?"

"There's no MLK to get shot, for one thing. And things are better, you know? Anyone can sit at whatever lunch counter they want."

Diego looked at me like I was too stupid even to feel sorry for. "E-man, where you been? There ain't no such thing as lunch counters anymore."

"Well, restaurant, then. You know what I mean. It's not like people aren't allowed to go places."

Diego shook his head.

"You don't need no laws to keep people out if people can't afford to go there," he said.

I didn't have an answer for that.

"I think there won't be more riots," he went on. "But not 'cause things is better, 'cause they worse."

"Worse than in 1968?"

"Hell, yeah! People's just as bad off, but now they ain't even organized enough to have a riot and make somebody pay attention. Now they too busy shooting themselves up or shooting each other up, so they just make it worse."

"So you think there should be riots?"

"Riots or something, yeah," he said.

The pictures in front of us started to look different to me. People weren't starting fires and looting stores for fun, I realized. Even though what they were doing was illegal, they had a purpose in mind.

"You know where I was that day I didn't go to the library?" Diego asked.

I didn't tell him I was glad he hadn't come, glad I got to kiss Sharita in the stairwell.

"No, where?" I said.

"I had to help my cousins move."

I waited for him to say more, but he didn't.

"But why — " I said.

"They had to move 'cause they got evicted, and they got evicted 'cause they complained too many times they didn't have no heat or hot water. The landlord found some rule about how many people could live there, but they didn't care about that rule for anybody else. They only cared because my cousins thought they should get the heat fixed. And I didn't break windows or nothing when I was helping them, but I wanted to, you know? I can understand what those riot people was probably thinking."

"That's — that's too bad. For your cousins, I mean."

"Yeah. We got all their stuff out, though. I know some other people got evicted and they just came home and found half their stuff sitting on the sidewalk. The other half was already gone."

"Man," I said.

"Yeah, so, do we got what we need for this project?"

We figured out that I would draw a map of where the riots took place and Diego would make a timeline of what happened when. For the rest of the period, we worked without talking.

《《　　》》

By four o'clock on Sunday afternoon, I couldn't put it off anymore. I had looked all over the house, even in the basement, but there was nothing like posterboard or magic markers anywhere. There was nowhere I could walk to get them, either. I had to ask my grandfather.

I waited for a commercial in the football game, but as soon as one came on my grandfather pulled his coupon-clipping scissors out of their case and squinted at the Sunday inserts.

"Uh, Grandpa?" I finally said.

He looked up quickly, like he didn't know where the

voice was coming from. When he saw it was me, he shook his head and said, "Didn't anyone teach you not to sneak up on a person?"

"Sorry."

"These coupons are very important," he said. "The manufacturers figure the amount of the coupon into their price, so they still make a profit on you. But if you buy the item without the coupon, you're subsidizing everyone who was smart enough to cut out the coupon. And who are they, that we should be subsidizing them?"

"Yeah." Outside, the sun was going down, and there was more light from the TV than from the window.

"What was it you wanted, that you scared me out of my chair like that?"

"Uh, it's about markers."

"Markers? Like in those spy movies, where they leave markers to show the other spies where they've been?"

"No, like magic markers."

"What about them?"

"I need some for my social studies project."

"Hmm," said my grandfather. "I think we've got an old laundry marker in the basement. I don't know if it writes, though."

"Well, actually, I need a whole set. For social studies, we have to make a map and color it different colors."

"Do you have to draw it on gilt-edged parchment, too?"

"No, just posterboard. Do we have any?"

"What does this school think we're running — an arts and crafts store?" My grandfather shook his head. "Next Saturday, if we have to, we'll make a trip to ValuBuy and get what you need."

The Redskins game came back on, and my grandfather put down his coupons like our conversation was over.

"Uh, one thing," I said.

He looked up at me.

"The project is sort of due before then."

"When is it sort of due?"

"Tomorrow?"

"Tomorrow! You expect me to miss the football game to buy you supplies for a project you've known about how long? I think you've got another think coming is what I think."

I was wondering if a person could fail social studies for coloring a map with a not-fully-working laundry marker (and if so, if their partner would fail social studies too) when my grandmother spoke up behind me. I hadn't even heard her come in.

"Oh, Ira, just take him to the CVS on Georgia Avenue."

"I don't think so," said my grandfather. "I think he should learn you can't just wait 'til the last — "

"I think you should learn that you can't make a federal

case every time you have to spend fifty cents on something. Besides, I'm out of my shampoo, and now you can take back that bottle that was the wrong kind."

My grandfather couldn't argue, since the shampoo problem had been his fault. He took me to CVS, and even though my stuff cost more than fifty cents, he didn't complain about paying for it. Dinner was a little more dried out than usual when we came back, but I didn't complain about that either.

The kitchen table was the only uncarpeted surface wide enough to spread the whole posterboard on at once. I was working on the map after dinner when my grandmother came in.

"Ethan?" she said. "Oh, that looks so nice."

At first I thought I was safe, that she hadn't noticed exactly what I was working on.

"Thanks," I said.

"Is that? . . . That looks like the area where your grandfather had his store."

"Yeah, we — I'm supposed to draw a map of where the 1968 riots took place."

"I see."

Then, still coloring, I asked her, "Why didn't you just move? You know, when all that stuff happened."

"Don't get me started."

But I wanted to get her started. I wanted to get something, or somebody started. I wanted to understand why my family was different, why my parents worked all the time, why they were getting divorced. And why I was really here, with the grandparents I hardly knew, eating dinner at four-thirty in the afternoon.

"I want to know," I said. "Moving would have solved everything for, like, three generations of people. Why didn't you just do it?"

"Moving doesn't solve everything," she said quietly. "When you move, you just bring the problem with you."

"Did Mom want to move?"

My grandmother sighed. "She *still* wants us to move. I don't think she'll ever give up. She's called us stubborn, cheap, and I don't even know what else, but here we are, still home."

Then my grandmother went upstairs to wash her hair with the new shampoo. *Still home.* Were my grandparents heroes? Cowards? Were they selfish? Or maybe they were just people, like anybody else. At least they knew where their home was, which was more than I could say. I looked at the map until the lines got blurry and the colors bled into each other. Then I yanked open a kitchen drawer, grabbed a rubber band from the top, and rolled up the map.

23

After talking to my mom and then my grandparents, everything was more intense, like I was noticing things around me for the first time. In jazz band especially, the oboe felt more solid in my hands, and the winter sun in the window made everyone's instruments look shinier. We played louder. The radiator steam and disinfectant in the band room smelled ten times as strong.

"Ethan," Mr. Harper said one day after school. "I think it's time."

I didn't know what he meant, but then he handed me a reed, and I saw it was a real one, made out of cane — no more beginner's plastic reed. He told me how it wouldn't work if it was too dry, or the wrong temperature, or even a little bit cracked.

"There's a lot more to watch out for," he said, "but it's worth it."

We only had two weeks until the concert. The gospel

choir was going to do a show before we played, and the step-dance club was going to perform afterward, so the audience would be bigger than it would have been just for the band. We decided that the concert would be free, but a table in the lobby would have information about Hungry for Music. We made a box for donations.

All the hallways had yellow flyers about the concert. Sharita read a "musical note" each day during morning announcements, which ended with a reminder about the concert. She was only late to school once the whole week.

The day before the concert, a few of us stayed after school to get ready. Someone's mother had photocopied the programs at her office, and now we had to fold them and stick in an insert listing everyone we wanted to thank.

"What are you doing over there — origami?" Anthony said when he saw me holding a program up, trying to refold it for the third or fourth time.

"Look, Ethan's making a origami," he said.

"Why don't you make us a string bass?" said Ngozi. "We could use one of those tomorrow."

I gave up. Since it had too many creases to be useful, I turned the program into a paper airplane and flew it at Ngozi, but it went too far and sailed into the open door of the room where we kept our instruments.

Sharita looked up from where she was painting a sign that said *Hungry? Buy a Brownie for Hungry for Music.*

"If you don't want to be here all night, could you *please* just fold the programs?" she said. "Ethan, why don't you stick the inserts in if folding is a problem?"

Now that it was winter, she sometimes wore stretchy socks that went all the way up under her pants. That day she was wearing one pink and orange stretchy sock and one that was bright purple, like her glasses.

Mr. Harper looked up from grading papers at his desk, but he shook his head and went back to work without saying anything.

Anthony said "Oooh," under his breath, but we listened to Sharita.

The music room was hot. Someone had opened a window to let some of the steam from the radiators escape, but it still felt more like May or June than December. My hands were sweaty, and a couple of the program inserts got wrinkled just from me touching them.

When we walked outside the school at 4:30, it was already getting dark.

"I can't believe it's tomorrow," Sharita said.

"Yeah."

"It's like, everything we've worked for is coming true."

"Yeah." I couldn't help it, I was looking at her. None of my friends back home would have thought she was pretty, not because she was black (at least they wouldn't have said so) but because she was smart and wore funny socks and had plans for herself. She put on her gloves, which were white with silver sparkles. When she looked back at me, she didn't look away.

Don't screw this up. Don't screw this up, don't screw this up, don't screw this up. That thought was so loud I missed what she was saying.

"Sorry?" I said.

Sharita sighed. "I *said,* are you okay getting home? Your grandparents won't be mad that it's dark?"

"Yeah, no, they're okay."

"That's good."

"You know," I said, "if I was older and had a car, I'd drive you home so you didn't have to take all those buses."

"Yeah?" She smiled. "What kind of car would you drive me home in?"

I thought quickly. "A red Porsche. With those seat warmers, so your butt doesn't get cold."

Sharita raised her eyebrows, and I thought she was mad at me for thinking about her butt, but she said, "Not in my neighborhood. Only a crazy person drives around a Porsche where I live. No seat warmers going to protect you there."

After Sharita got on the bus, I couldn't stop thinking about her. Not only was she smart and beautiful, but she had gotten this concert organized, so whatever elementary kids started playing an instrument instead of getting in trouble had Sharita to thank. I might have been imagining it, but it seemed like kids were avoiding her less in the halls, giving each other fewer looks when she came late to school. Or maybe Sharita was just acting like they were doing that, which came out the same thing. It was good that Mr. Harper had given us the night off from practicing our instruments, because I couldn't have focused that night even if I wanted to.

◀◀◀   ▶▶▶

The next morning, I woke up with a single thought: *Tonight I'll be performing in front of my biggest audience ever.* Most kids still didn't know me, but they recognized me every time I walked down the hall. I couldn't mess up. I had to be perfect.

At breakfast, between bites of cereal, I held my spoon with two hands, going over the fingering for my solo.

"Trying to squeeze in a little extra practice before the concert?" my grandfather asked.

"No . . . Well, I guess."

"So what time is this concert?" my grandmother asked.

I swallowed some milk.

"I don't know. Seven, I think." Then I saw her look at my grandfather and I added quickly, "But you don't have to come! I mean, you'd miss *Jeopardy!* and everything."

"Don't be silly," my grandmother said, "of course we'll be there."

"But — "

My grandfather interrupted.

"What do you think — we're going to make ourselves noticed by clapping at the wrong time? We know not to clap between movements."

He smiled. Even if they clapped at the right times, the only thing more obvious than me in the jazz band would be a couple of white-haired Jewish grandparents at an all-black Christmas concert.

"You're not going to like the music," I said. "It's going to be Christmas stuff. And not just Rudolph the Red-Nosed Reindeer. I mean, like, Jesus songs."

This time of year, my mom would always change the radio station when Jesus songs came on, but my grandmother just sniffed. "We used to go to those every year, until our neighbor's little girl graduated high school. Just because it's not *our* music doesn't mean we can't enjoy it."

"Whatever," I mumbled. I stood up and walked away from the table.

"Ethan," my grandmother called after me. "I know if that spoon were a real oboe we wouldn't think about loading it into the dishwasher — "

I went back and put my dirty dishes away.

In math first period, I was doing the same thing with

my pencil, holding it straight up and practicing the fingering like it was an oboe. This was stupid. I had never been
this nervous about a concert before. But I had to make a
special effort to show I was as good as anyone else.

Between classes, I left Sharita a note in her locker that
was just a note, a picture of a musical note drawn on a corner of a sheet of notebook paper. I knew she would know
it was from me. I could usually open my locker on the first
try now, and when I opened my locker at lunchtime, I
found a folded-up sheet of paper with a circle drawn on
the outside. On the inside, she had written, *Why did you
only leave me a quarter note? For you, here's a whole note.* She
signed it with a heart, comma, *Sharita.*

Heart, comma, Sharita.

I wrote one other note that day too. It was my dad's
birthday, so even though I knew the mail wouldn't get
there in time, I folded a piece of notebook paper in half
and drew a birthday cake that had musical instruments as
candles.

Inside I wrote, "Dear Dad, Happy birthday. Tonight
I'm playing in my first oboe concert. Maybe after I come
home I'll play for you sometime, if you have an oboe I can
borrow. Your son, Ethan."

After I wrote the message, I looked at the picture again.
Something was missing. Finally, in each corner I drew a
chicken playing an oboe. I doubted he would pick up on

the chicken soup reference (if that was even who my grandparents were talking about that day, my dad driving chicken soup to my mom when she was away at school) but I didn't want to ask for sure and risk having it not be true. Maybe some part of my dad's subconscious would see the chickens playing the oboe and want to be that person again.

All day the music kept going around and around in my head, louder than whatever the teacher was saying and the body noises of the kids around me. It was louder than worries about my family or Maple Heights or anything else that was usually important. For one day, music was everything.

‹‹‹ ›››

Since we had to be back at school by six o'clock, Mr. Harper got pizzas for us. No soda, though, so we wouldn't burp during the concert. At four-thirty, Anthony and Ngozi and I had a contest to see who could gargle water the longest without laughing and spitting it back into their plastic cup. At five-thirty, all the boys crowded around the sink in the bathroom, brushing our teeth (a condition of being allowed to eat pizza before the concert). And at six-thirty, we filed into the auditorium, sitting on stage on cold metal chairs and feeling about five years older. I barely even noticed my hurting feet in the dress shoes. Our music took on a serious tone just from being on stage. I wished I had practiced more.

After the music started, most of the night was a blur. I thought I saw my grandparents come in, but then I wasn't sure it was them. But then I figured, what other old white people would be at this concert? During the gospel choir, I was too busy going over my music in my head to be nervous about what my grandparents were thinking about the gospel songs.

The band part of the concert was even more of a blur. Playing music was just something my body did, like breathing, which gets weird and hard to do if you think about it too much.

So I didn't think. I just played.

I was the fifth solo out of six. When it was my turn, I took a deep breath, and then my lips and fingers did the rest. I had stopped being afraid of what words might fill my head to go along with what the oboe playing. Or, with its grown-up reed, singing.

I am Ethan (I heard in my head, almost like I was doing a tap dance),

I like junk food (tappity-tap, tap, tap),

And making people laugh (tap-tap-tap)

And playing music with pretty girls (tappity-tap, sliiiiide).

I'm not perfect (tap, tap),

But what's "perfect," anyway? (tap, tap),

Ignore me at your peril. (tappity-tap, tappity-tap, the
  end!)

When I finished, there was a pause, and I imagined the audience taking it in, people thinking, "Oh. That's who that white kid is. I had wondered about him." Then Ngozi had his solo and we went on with the rest of "Boogie Woogie Christmas."

I breezed through the rest of the concert, counting out the rhythm in my head, and wiping the sweat off my palms. It felt like we were up there about five seconds before the audience was clapping and it was time to go to our special seats in the first two rows of the audience. Looking up, with my head resting against the back of the seat, the kids in step club looked like graceful giants, weaving their separate rhythms into the changing rhythm of the group. At one point I closed my eyes and just listened to their shoes hitting the stage.

I wasn't ready for it to end. I took as long as possible packing up my oboe. Eventually, my grandparents found me in the lobby, and my grandfather gave me a sort-of hug, the first one he had given me since I came to Washington. "Not half bad," he said. "I didn't even have to use the earplugs your grandmother had me bring."

My grandmother hit him lightly on the arm.

"Don't listen to him, Ethan," she said. "You were wonderful. You didn't tell us you were going to have a solo."

I tried to sound casual. "I didn't know how it was going to go, so I didn't want you to get your hopes up."

My grandfather said, "Ethan, my hopes for you have been up since the day you were born. As soon as they called to say you were a boy, and not only that but you spit up on the idiot doctor who delivered you, I said, 'I'm pinning my hopes on that one.'"

I didn't know I had spit up on an idiot doctor, but that night felt like the ultimate spitting up on all the idiots in the world, all the people back in Maple Heights, everyone who didn't think I was worth paying attention to.

I am Ethan. Ignore me at your peril.

24

I didn't want the high to end. I wanted to take all the money we raised for Hungry for Music, buy instruments that weekend, and force them on disadvantaged kids by Monday. Everyone should get to be in a concert like that, I thought. Anyone who ever thought or wondered what playing an instrument in front of people was like. But on Sunday night, I thought of one person in particular: Diego.

The idea seemed better the more I thought about it. Diego was older than most kids who started an instrument, but he could catch up. Maybe he could be like Mr. Harper. Like, if his parents couldn't afford to send Diego and all of his siblings to college, Diego's instrument could send him to college. It was so simple I couldn't believe I hadn't thought of it sooner. It didn't matter anymore if Diego wanted to be my friend, or even if he forgave me for whatever stupid things I had said about everyone having all the civil rights they needed. I had thought of a way to make it up to him — more than make it up to him, even.

Monday morning though, Diego wasn't in any of our classes. By lunchtime, I wasn't so sure it was a great idea. I had learned that not everything that made sense in my head made sense at Parker Junior High. I had to tell him about Hungry for Music before I talked myself out of it.

At Diego's lunch table, Johnny had two strawberry ice cream sticks on his tray and one in his mouth. José was drinking Mountain Dew. They looked up at me but didn't say anything. José wiggled the tab on his Mountain Dew can and pulled it off like a loose tooth.

"Hey," I said.

"Hey." Johnny snapped his gum.

"Uh, so — " I hadn't rehearsed this part, how to talk to Diego's friends and sound casual. "So, where's Diego?"

Johnny looked up at me like I had asked him to pull Diego out from under the table.

José kept a cool expression on his face. "Don't tell me you were part of this one too."

"Part of what?" I said.

Johnny broke one of the Popsicle sticks from his ice cream bar in half. I felt like I had no knees. "I think he really don't know."

"Don't know what?" I said. What happened to Diego?

"He got suspended," said José.

Johnny added, "Maybe expelled."

"They don't know yet," José explained. "He got in a fight yesterday on the parking lot. If it's drugs, he could get expelled."

"Wow."

"If it's only suspended, it's not too bad, but if it's expelled, he's gotta go to, like, a special school and everything."

"He might not ever come back," said Johnny, and José gave him a look.

Had anyone talked about me like that when I got suspended from Maple Heights Middle School?

I wished I had thought of this plan last Friday. Then maybe Diego could have been choosing an instrument over the weekend, not getting into fights. I was sure I had the solution to his problems, if only I could reach him.

"Do you have his phone number?" I blurted out.

"What you need his phone number for?" said José.

"I gotta tell him something."

"Well, I don't think his phone's working this month. You got a problem with that?"

"No. No problem." Some people's phones worked some months and not others, depending on when they could pay. I didn't know that before I came here.

"I guess you don't — I guess there's no other way to reach him."

José had a cold look on his face, like he was about ten years older. "Nope."

What would I have said to Diego, anyway? "Call this number so you can play a musical instrument and turn your life around"? When would I learn to mind my own business? There was nothing left to say.

"Oh. Well, thanks," I said, but José and Johnny didn't answer.

I took my lunch to the staircase and sat on the bottom step. My lunch smelled like the lotion my grandmother was wearing when she first stuffed the plastic bag into the old Kleenex box. Today was tuna fish on wheat with a mushy banana.

After lunch, I found out that Diego and I got an A- on our social studies project. I tried sending him a telepathic message to come back to school. "See?" I told him silently, wherever he was. "You don't even have to play an instrument if you don't want to. You could go to college on a social studies scholarship." If he heard me, he didn't send a telepathic message back.

In band, we learned that our concert had raised $384 for Hungry for Music. According to Mr. Harper's friend, that was enough to send two kids to music camp for a week, or cover the rental of a trumpet, a trombone, and a clarinet for one year.

Mr. Harper said he was proud of us, and he added, "I

hope this is only the beginning of a lifetime spent using music to enrich the world. To that end, what would you think about planning a second community music night at the end of the school year?"

He had barely asked the question before kids started jumping to get involved. Kids who hadn't been part of the planning for the first concert saw what a big deal it turned into, and they wanted to be in on the next one.

A kid named Khalif, who designed the concert programs and some of the flyers, raised his hand and asked, "Maybe we could do a whole community arts night? Have the music concert, but also give the art kids a chance to have an exhibit."

"Can we have a talent show?"

"Can we invite those kids who do break-dancing? That's a talent, right?"

Ideas piled on top of each other, until it sounded like Friday night's concert would be nothing compared with the big deal event in the spring. Would I even be here in the spring? I mostly kept quiet, except for agreeing to Khalif's idea and a few other ideas that sounded good.

‹‹‹   ›››

That night, after the news, my grandfather turned to *Jeopardy!*

"Elementary school week," he said with a sneer. "Little

248

pipsqueak from North Dakota won about a million dollars last night and didn't even look like he was old enough to put his own pants on."

"Ira," my grandmother said, looking up from her crossword puzzle.

"Well, he didn't. Ethan could have answered more questions than he did if Ethan didn't have better things to do with his time."

"Like play award-winning oboe solos," my grandmother said, looking at me.

"That's what I mean, things like that."

"Actually, I don't have much going on tonight," I said. When they looked at me, I added, "You know, end of school, getting ready for winter break and all. Maybe I'll stick around for *Jeopardy!*"

My grandfather beamed like I had just gotten a full scholarship to Harvard Pharmacy School and offered to reopen his store. He motioned me over to his chair and showed me the piece of paper on his lap. Leaning against the TV listings, he was writing on the back of a piece of junk mail.

"Now here's where we write down our score," he said. "Either of us gets the right answer, it counts, even if the other one gets it wrong. All the daily doubles are true daily doubles, no penalty for guessing wrong. When it's time for Final Jeopardy, we write the other fellows' scores in these boxes, we write our answer over here, and here's where we write our final score. If you — ssh! They're starting."

"Okay," I said, fighting the urge to laugh.

The pipsqueak from North Dakota was back, along with a tall, skinny girl and a boy whose ears stuck out. Two of the categories were made for me: "Musical Instruments" and "Philadelphia." But just as the boy whose ears stuck out was selecting the first question, the phone rang.

My grandmother answered the phone from the dark wood doily-covered table next to the couch, even though my grandfather was signaling that she shouldn't talk there or we'd miss the show.

"Hello?" she said.

Part of me knew even then what was happening.

"Mm-hmm," she said. "Well, fine, thanks. We got hit pretty hard with that snow. Mm-hmm, yes, he's right here."

My grandfather waved his arms and shook his head, like saying he wasn't home, but my grandmother told me, "Ethan, your mother's on the phone. Why don't you take it in the kitchen so your grandfather can watch his show?"

I walked into the kitchen, but not quickly, and picked up the receiver.

"Hello?" I said.

My grandmother hung up.

"Hi, sweetie," said my mom.

"Hi."

My mom never called me "sweetie" when something good was happening. It was never, "Good work, sweetie!" or "Way to go, sweetie!" "Sweetie" was a way of softening things, like when she said, "Sweetie, I didn't mean for you to find out like this" about the end of her marriage. Or when she said at the train station, "I know it's going to be hard, sweetie, but it's only for a little while."

I was about to find out exactly how long a little while was.

"Ethan, honey, listen. These past few months have been — I've put a lot of pieces back together."

"That's good."

"Thanks for understanding," she said. "This may sound silly, but I'm finally ready to be a mom again."

"You were always a mom," I said. I meant it in a sarcastic, duh, what-else-were-you way, but I think she took it in a sappy greeting card way.

"If you come home during winter break, we'll have a little time to catch up before things get crazy with school again."

Winter break? That was too soon. I tried to remember everything I missed about Maple Heights, besides eating normal food and playing clarinet. But instead I kept thinking, *I don't want to go.*

"Listen, you know how your PlayStation hadn't been

251

working? Well, this morning's paper had a coupon for Circuit Circus, ten percent off on repairs. So I brought it in at lunchtime, and they said they'll fix it by the end of the week. Isn't that great? I was going to leave it as a surprise for when you got here, but then I thought you'd enjoy looking forward to it."

"Thanks," I said, because it was nice of her to do that for me, especially when I was the one who broke it (even though she didn't exactly know that part). I knew she didn't mean it as a bribe, like come back to live here and you can play all the video games you want. My video game-playing self seemed like another person now. Did I even want to go home? Couldn't I bring the PlayStation to Washington?

"Um, about the PlayStation . . ." I said.

"Uh huh?"

"Nothing. I mean, thanks for getting it fixed."

"You're welcome. I'll see you soon, sweetie. Love you!"

"Love you too," I said, but I couldn't tell whether she had already hung up.

Something was wrong with me. Why wasn't I jumping at the chance to go home as soon as possible? I remembered my first day at Parker, and how I would have rather clipped a million coupons than gone to school here. Now I was being set free; I should be jumping around the room, throwing a party. Instead, I ripped out a sheet of notebook paper and leaned it against a Lone Ranger comic book. Then I made two lists, reasons to stay here a while and reasons to go home.

Reasons to stay in Washington for a while
1. Kids in Maple Heights who used to be my friends but who hadn't written or called the whole time I was in D.C. (people who would make Sharita uncomfortable if I somehow brought her to Maple Heights Middle School for the end-of-the-year eighth grade dance).
2. Sharita, Diego (if he came back), and Felix and Daron (if my grandfather would drive me to Maryland).
3. The oboe, which I would forget how to play if I didn't practice.
4. My grandparents, who eat weird food, but who eat dinner with me every single night (or afternoon). Okay, four-thirty is a little weird, but it's nice having someone pay attention to my life.
5. If I moved during the summer, I could easily explain, "I spent the year in D.C. with my grandparents" rather than changing schools twice in one year and making people think something was wrong.

Reasons to go home
1. My non-saggy bed.
2. Computer with Internet connection.

3. Vietnamese food, Fruit-by-the-Foot, and every other kind of normal food I ate at home.

4. It would be hard to tell my mom I was staying after she had the PlayStation fixed.

5. I'd get to see Margo when she came home for winter break.

6. In 1968, my grandparents stayed in their home even when it would have been easier to live elsewhere. Maybe going home was what I had to do, even if it wasn't easy.

25

On my last morning in Washington, I ate a bowl of oatmeal and two bananas while I listened to my grandparents
argue about parking near Union Station.

"You park on Second Street, you can stay up to two
hours before they make you move the car."

"Second Street? You're going to have us climbing over
snow banks?" my grandmother said.

"Why own boots if you can't walk through a little
snow?"

"You walk through snow when you have to, not so you
can park six blocks away to save fifty cents."

"Fifty cents? You think that's how much parking costs,
fifty cents?"

My duffel bag was packed and waiting on my uncle's
bed. It had a few more things than when I got here, but
not many: a couple of letters from Margo, a program from
our music concert, my riot map rolled up with a rubber

band, and a picture of Sharita that she had left in my locker on my last day at Parker.

I was looking out the window, wondering what to do for two and a half hours on the train, when a familiar-looking car turned onto our street and parked in front of my grandparents' house.

Out of the car stepped my mom.

She was wearing her black coat and carrying a shiny red purse she used for work. I opened the front door and met her outside before she rang the bell.

When I hugged her, her coat smelled clean, like she had just gotten it back from the dry cleaner, and her hair smelled like her shampoo. I had missed that smell without knowing it. She had a gray hair I had never noticed just above her ear.

We stood there a minute before my mom said, "So, should we get you inside?"

Just like when Felix came over, I was standing there without a coat or shoes on.

"Sure."

Inside, I started to call, "Grandpa, we don't have to drive to the tr — " when I saw my grandparents had come downstairs.

"Susan? You didn't have to drive all the way down here," my grandmother said, but she was smiling.

My grandfather smiled too. "Did you hit a lot of traffic on I-95?"

My mom smiled back. Other than the band concert, when was the last time I was in a room with three smiling people?

"No, not much. I left early," she said.

My grandfather nodded. "Good thinking. Did you use the detour in Delaware? To miss the toll?"

My mom closed her eyes briefly. "No, Dad. I was kind of anxious to see my son." And my coupon-clipping grandfather just nodded.

My mom came upstairs with me to get my stuff, even though I said I could carry it down. She opened the door to her old room and shut it again without going in. But in my uncle's room, she stood for a minute in the middle of the room, her eyes closed, just breathing.

At first I thought it was weird, but then I realized maybe she could answer something that was still hanging over me.

"Mom?"

"Mm-hmm?"

"When Uncle Ed died, was he — I mean, I know he had a bad reaction to some medicine, but was he, you know . . ."

My mom opened her eyes. "You mean, was he on drugs?"

I nodded.

My mom sat down on the edge of the bed.

"Probably," she said. "He died when he was on the way to Mississippi for his 'freedom ride.' Hard to believe how someone could fight for what's right and act so crazy at the same time."

But I didn't find it hard to believe at all.

We didn't stay around long, because we had to get home in time for Margo's plane, but my mom said since Margo had a six-week vacation, the three of us could drive down to visit D.C. in January.

So when I hugged my grandparents goodbye, it wasn't all dramatic; it was more like "See you in a few weeks." That was how I imagined normal families said goodbye to grandparents.

"Make sure you show your mother that concert program," said my grandmother.

"You did good, kiddo," my grandfather said.

As we pulled onto the highway, I told my mom, "My friend Diego would like this trip. He wants to go to all fifty states."

"Do you have his phone number?" my mom said. "Maybe he could visit this summer."

"No, he — never mind," I said.

For a while I closed my eyes and in my head I played "In the Mood" on the oboe, the fingering and everything.

It sounded pretty good in my head, and I thought about playing it for my family at home until I remembered I didn't play the oboe anymore. I opened my eyes. "My" oboe was in the band room at Parker Junior High, in Washington D.C., getting further and further away. Back home was my clarinet, which I still liked, but it wasn't special the way an oboe was. Half the band at Maple Heights Middle School played clarinets and trumpets, but I was the only person I knew who played oboe.

After an hour, I was starving. I knew my mom would stop for fast food if I wanted, but I was curious about the lunch my grandmother had packed when we thought I was taking the train. She wouldn't make my lunch again for a long time, maybe ever. This would be the last time I'd open a crinkled plastic bag from Safeway and find an old-people lunch of something on rye bread wrapped in a used plastic baggie. I decided to enjoy this last one.

The Safeway bag was lighter than I expected. My grandmother knew how much I ate, and she knew I'd be starving on the train. But the bag weighed almost nothing.

The only thing inside was an envelope. Great, her last chance to put a note in my lunch, like my mom did when I was little, telling me she loved me or whatever, only she forgot the food!

Inside the envelope, my grandmother had left a note, but she also left a ten-dollar bill. Ten dollars! That would have been more than enough for lunch on the train. The note said, in my grandmother's loopy handwriting:

December 21

Dear Ethan,

I know you wanted to buy your lunch at the school cafeteria, but your grandfather and I saw it as throwing good money away. We didn't want to set you up for a bad habit. But since the train is not a habit, it didn't seem like much harm if you bought your lunch this time. Hopefully this will cover it.

Love,

Grandma

Then, on the next line, my grandfather had added "and Grandpa" in his own handwriting. He had probably never paid ten dollars for lunch in his whole life. I must have read that note five or six times, and every time I smiled when I got to where my grandfather had signed it.

I treated my mom to (most of) our lunch at Roy Rogers along the highway. That was where my mom told me that my dad wanted my sister and me to visit his new apartment during winter break. It was up to us, she said, if we wanted to go.

I had forgotten the size of my bathroom at home, and the good water pressure, and the name-brand shampoo. After my shower, I had just finished getting dressed when my mom knocked on my door.

"Ethan, you had a phone message."

Already? Who knew I was here, except —

"This boy was talking so fast I almost couldn't understand him," my mom said, and then I knew. "He said his name is Felix, and you can call him back tonight in Maryland. Do you know who that is?"

"Yeah, it's Felix Taylor, the guy who used to live next door to Grandma and Grandpa." He must have called my grandmother for the number in Pennsylvania. I wondered if my grandmother had interrogated him or made him hold on while she turned down the volume on the television.

"Oh, those poor Taylor boys," my mom said. "Let me see what else he said."

She looked at the notepaper in her hand. "He said he got our number from Grandma and Grandpa, and they also insisted on giving our address because they told him it was cheaper to write a letter."

I smiled.

"He also said to tell you he's getting an email address

soon but he doesn't have it yet, and you should wait to call back because they're going out for ice cream." She paused. "I think that was it."

I would have a lot to tell Felix later. And Margo. We still had an hour before we had to meet her plane, so I stretched out on my bed, feeling the firm mattress under my back and the smooth comforter under my fingers. I looked at the glow-in-the-dark stars on my ceiling like some other kid had stuck them there a hundred years ago. My grandparents would be getting ready for dinner soon. I could still feel the Roy Rogers lunch in my stomach, but I was starting to get hungry again.

From the front pocket of my duffel bag, I took out my picture of a grinning Sharita. She had kissed me on the left cheek when she gave it to me, a leaving-the-possibilities-open kiss that I could still feel when I closed my eyes.

I reached under the bed and found a notebook with a pen stuck in the spiral. I pulled the pen out and wrote:

Dear Sharita,

Thanks for the picture of you. It's on my dresser right now. We had school pictures taken before I left Maple Heights Middle School, so if I ever get them back and they don't look stupid, maybe I'll send you one. I'm glad we got to work together on the Hungry for Music concert.

Speaking of hungry, we are going out for Vietnamese food tonight after we pick up my sister. Have you ever tried a barbecue pork bun?

The ride home was okay. My room is like I remember it, but my PlayStation works now. My mom said we're going to visit in January, when my sister is home from school, so if you're not busy, maybe I'll see you then.

In case you want to write back, my address is on the outside of the envelope.

I hesitated at the end of the letter, and finally I wrote, "Your friend, Ethan." Then I stood up. I couldn't remember where we kept the stamps and envelopes.

On the way out of my room, I saw a heavy black box on the floor next to my bookcase. I had almost forgotten: my clarinet. I put Sharita's letter down and sat on the floor. The clarinet pieces fit together stiffly.

The oboe had felt so light at first, but I got used to it, and now the clarinet felt heavier than I remembered. I held it for a minute or so, and then I blew into it. The sound was more mellow than the oboe, less complicated. I played a few notes and then realized they were the first few notes of "In the Mood." It was in a different key and sounded weird, but I kept playing anyway. I could hear the other kids in the band around me. I could see Sharita's wild-colored socks, and I could taste the chicken salad sandwich I would have just eaten for lunch.

After putting the clarinet away, I picked up Sharita's letter again and added a quick P.S. *I just finished playing "In the Mood" on the clarinet, and it was okay. If you want, tell me what time you practice your trombone and it can be like we're playing a duet.*

I hesitated, wondering if that last line sounded stupid, but then I tore the letter out of the notebook and folded it up.

Margo would be proud: I had finally written a letter. Actually, I had done a lot of things that I wouldn't have thought possible while living in a time-warp world with my grandparents. I had snuck out to spy on a neighbor, taken a bus by myself to Maryland, kissed a girl, played an instrument most kids have barely heard of, and learned a few things about my family.

What would be next? Fixing things with Alex Krashevsky, hopefully, and maybe figuring out which of my former friends in Maple Heights might still be my friends. But for now I was starving. How many foods that I missed from Maple Heights could I cross off with one snack?

We still had half an hour before we had to leave for the airport. Plenty of time to find out.

Author's Note

Want to read more about it?

There's plenty of information about civil rights, available on the Internet or at your local library. Here are some resources I found helpful in writing this book:

Gilbert, Ben W. *Ten blocks from the White House: Anatomy of the Washington riots of 1968*. New York: F. A. Praeger, 1968.

Smith, Kathryn Schneider. *Washington at home: An illustrated history of neighborhoods in the nation's capital*. Northridge California, Windsor Publications, 1988.

Caplan, Marvin. *Farther Along: A Civil Rights Memoir*. Baton Rouge: Louisiana State Univ Press, 1999.

The Civil Rights Movement Veterans website offers a bibliography of resources for young readers. Visit www.crmvet.org/biblio.htm.

Want to do more about it?

Hungry for Music
This organization mentioned in the book actually exists and operates in Washington, D.C. For more information, visit www.hungryformusic.com.

The Public Education Network (PEN)
PEN seeks to create quality public education for all children. For suggestions about how students can improve public school systems for themselves and others, visit www.publiceducation.org/getinvolved.asp.

The National Coalition Building Institute
This international, non-profit, leadership training organization based in Washington, D.C., works to eliminate racism and all other forms of prejudice and discrimination throughout the world. For more information, visit www.ncbi.org.